THE CAVE OF THE DARK WIND

A NEVER LAND BOOK

DAVE BARRY is a Pulitzer Prize-winning humorist whose column appears in more than five hundred newspapers in the USA and abroad. He is the author of more than twenty books, including *Boogers Are My Beat*, *Dave Barry's Complete Guide to Guys* and *Big Trouble*, several of which have been adapted for cinema and TV. Written in collaboration with longtime friend Ridley Pearson, the *New York Times* Best Seller *Peter and the Starcatchers* was Dave Barry's first foray into children's literature, followed by *Peter and the Shadow Thieves* and *Peter and the Secret of Rundoon*. Dave Barry lives in Miami, USA, with his wife, Michelle, and his children, Rob and Sophie.

RIDLEY PEARSON is a bestselling crime novelist whose work includes *The Diary of Ellen Rimbauer*, *The First Victim* and *Parallel Lies*. In 1991, he was the first American to be awarded the Raymond Chandler/Fulbright Fellowship in Detective Fiction at Oxford University. Ridley Pearson also plays bass guitar in the literary all-star garage band, the Rock Bottom Remainders. The band is comprised of some of America's most popular writers, including Dave Barry and Stephen King. Ridley Pearson lives with his wife, Marcelle, and their two daughters, Paige and Storey, dividing their time between the Northern Rockies and the Midwest.

NEVER LAND

THE CAVE OF THE DARK WIND

By DAVE BARRY
and RIDLEY PEARSON

Illustrations by GREG CALL

WALKER
BOOKS

First published in Great Britain 2008 by Walker Books Ltd
87 Vauxhall Walk, London SE11 5HJ

2 4 6 8 10 9 7 5 3 1

Text © 2007 Dave Barry and Page One, Inc.
Illustrations © 2007 Greg Call

The moral rights of Dave Barry, Ridley Pearson and Greg Call
have been asserted by them in accordance with the
Copyright, Designs and Patents Act 1988

This book has been typeset in Goudy

Printed and bound in Great Britain
by Creative Print and Design (Wales), Ebbw Vale

British Library Cataloguing in Publication Data: a catalogue record for this
book is available from the British Library

ISBN 978-1-4063-0731-3

www.walkerbooks.co.uk

Dear Reader—

A little while back we wrote a book called *Peter and the Starcatchers*. It told the story of what happened to Peter Pan *before* he was Peter Pan and how he became a boy who could fly.

That book ended with Peter and his friends on an island with mermaids, pirates, and some natives who call themselves the Mollusk tribe.

Right now, Peter is off having more adventures, and we're writing other books about those. But while he's gone, exciting things are happening to his friends—and his enemies—on the island. We decided it would be fun to tell some of those stories in books for younger readers (like our own children). And so we wrote the book you're holding now. We hope you enjoy reading it as much as we enjoyed writing it.

Sincerely,

Dave Barry and Ridley Pearson

TABLE OF CONTENTS

CHAPTER 1
A BAD IDEA

Six children—two girls and four boys—were toiling slowly up the side of a hill. It was a sticky, hot day on Mollusk Island, and the going was hard—the hill steep and thick with jungle plants. The children swatted at big, ugly bugs that hummed and buzzed while looking for a landing place, and maybe a biting place. The air smelled of wet soil and decay. From the jungle around them came the screeches of monkeys and birds and other unseen creatures.

"How much farther?" shouted Tubby Ted, who trudged along, last in line. Tubby Ted was almost always last, except when the line was for food.

"Just a little more!" answered Shining Pearl from the front of the line, where she led the way. Behind her, scrambling to keep up with her big sister, came Little Scallop. The girls both had sea green eyes and wore their black hair long—Shining Pearl's twisted into a thick braid, Little Scallop's pulled into a ponytail. They both knew the island well; their father, Fighting Prawn, was chief of the Mollusk tribe, which had lived here for centuries.

Behind Little Scallop followed James, the youngest but most daring of the bunch, then Prentiss, who would have been the teacher's pet had there been a school, which luckily there wasn't. After him came Thomas, whose curly brown hair blew around in the wind and, behind them—far behind them—Tubby Ted.

They called themselves the Lost Boys. Usually they were led by Peter, who was very brave and could also fly. But right now, Peter was off in England, visiting his friend Molly. And when Peter was gone, James was the leader. At least *he* thought he was. Not everybody followed him all the time.

It had been James's idea to climb this hill. The

children had been playing near Mermaid Lagoon, holding snake races, but eventually they had grown bored with that. The snakes refused to go in a straight line, so it was impossible to say who had won the race. Tired of arguing about this, the children finally gave up. They were sitting around, staring at the unbelievably blue water, when James made a proposal.

"Let's go exploring," he said.

"But Peter told us to stay near the lagoon," protested Prentiss. "He doesn't want us going near the pirates while he's away."

The pirates, led by Captain Hook, lived in a log fort on the other side of Mollusk Island. They pretty much stayed away from the side where the boys lived, because the boys lived in a thatch hut near the Mollusk village. The Mollusks protected the boys from Hook, who did not like people in general and *especially* did not like the Lost Boys.

"I know," said James, "but Peter could be gone for weeks. I don't want to spend *weeks* sitting here, do you?"

The other boys shook their heads.

"Besides," James continued, "there are lots of places we can explore that are nowhere near the pirate fort. Isn't that right, Shining Pearl?"

"Yes," she said.

"Like that hill above your village," said Thomas. "What's up there?"

Instead of answering him, Shining Pearl exchanged a look with Little Scallop.

"Why are you looking at each other that way?"

asked James. "What's up that hill?"

"Goat Meadow," answered Shining Pearl.

"Are there really goats up there?" asked Prentiss.

"Oh, yes," said Shining Pearl. She hesitated. "And something else."

"Like what?" said James.

Shining Pearl pursed her lips, clearly reluctant to answer.

"A . . . cave," said Little Scallop. This drew an anxious look from her older sister.

James's face lit up. "A cave?" he said. "Let's go!"

Shining Pearl looked worried. "I don't think we should," she said.

"Why not?" asked James. "It'll be an adventure!" He was already thinking about how he'd tell Peter all about it, when Peter came back from London.

"We're not supposed to go near the cave," said Shining Pearl.

"Why not?" said James.

Another look passed between the two girls, then Shining Pearl spoke.

"It's dangerous," she said.

"What's dangerous about it?" said James.

"You'll make fun of me if I tell you," said Shining

Pearl. She liked James, but he *did* tend to tease her.

"I promise I won't," James said.

"Yes, you will," she said.

"Well, can we at least go and *look* at the cave?" said James. "From the outside? What harm can that do?"

"We're not supposed to go near it," said Little Scallop.

"All right, then," said James. "If you two want to stay down here, fine. But I want to have a look at that cave. Who's with me?"

Prentiss and Thomas nodded, followed, reluctantly, by Tubby Ted.

"We're off, then," said James, starting up the path that led away from the lagoon.

"Wait!" said Shining Pearl.

James turned and looked at her. "What?" he said.

Shining Pearl sighed. "All right," she said. "I'll take you up there."

"We shouldn't!" objected Little Scallop.

"I know we shouldn't!" snapped Shining Pearl. "You're the one who got us into this!" she reminded her. "But now we have to go. There's no telling what trouble they'll get themselves into on their own."

She turned to James. "If I show you where the cave is, will you promise to do as I say?"

"Of course!" said James, grinning. "Don't I always?"

"No," answered Shining Pearl.

"Well, this time I will," said James, still grinning.

"You'd better," said Shining Pearl. "Follow me." She strode past James and started up the path, muttering to herself.

"This is a bad idea," she said. "A *very* bad idea."

CHAPTER 2

THE GOAT TAKER

"WE'RE HERE!" shouted Shining Pearl, as she finally reached the top of the hill. "Goat Meadow!"

One by one, the other five stumbled out of the thick jungle that covered the hillside and into a large clearing, blanketed with shin-high grass. Tubby Ted was the last to arrive, staggering over the crest of the hill and immediately sprawling on the ground, pressing his beetroot red face into the soft grass.

"I'm never going to walk anywhere again," he declared.

"Really?" said James.

"Really," said Ted.

"Then you're going to get eaten by a goat," said James.

"WHAT? HEY!" said Ted, looking up, then leaping to his feet. "GET AWAY!"

Ted was addressing a nanny goat that appeared to be quite interested in his trousers. The others laughed as Ted shooed the goat away. The goat had a kind of bell around her neck, made from a coconut shell; it clattered when she moved. She stopped several feet from Ted, eyeing him curiously.

"You can't blame her for wanting to taste your trousers," said Shining Pearl, giggling. "It must be awfully boring, eating grass day after day."

Looking around the meadow, the children saw that there were perhaps a hundred goats of various ages, some watching them, some grazing contentedly, the younger ones frolicking.

"How did they get onto this island?" asked Prentiss.

"The same way you did," said Shining Pearl. "They were shipwrecked."

"When?" said Thomas.

"Oh, a long time ago," said Shining Pearl. "Before I was born, and before my parents were born. There were no human survivors, just a few goats. They wandered until they found this meadow, and there have been goats here ever since. There were just a few at first, but the herd has grown, with the help of my people."

"What kind of help?" asked James.

"We keep an eye out for animals that might eat them," said Shining Pearl. "Big snakes, mostly."

The boys nodded; Mollusk Island had snakes as fat as tree trunks, snakes that could make a quick snack of a goat.

Tubby Ted stood up quickly, looking around for snakes.

"And if a bad storm comes," continued Shining Pearl, "we herd the goats under the trees at the end of the meadow. It's not easy, getting all these goats in one place."

"Why do you go to all that trouble?" said Prentiss.

"Yes," said Thomas, "I mean, they're only goats."

"Well," said Shining Pearl, "one reason is that they give us milk, which we drink and use to make cheese."

"Cheese?" said Tubby Ted, perking up. "Where?"

"Not here," said Shining Pearl, smiling. "We

make it in the village."

"What else?" said James.

"What do you mean?" said Shining Pearl.

"You said the milk was one reason. What's another reason?"

Again, Shining Pearl hesitated. Again she looked at Little Scallop.

"Tell them," said Little Scallop. "Then they'll know why we shouldn't be up here."

"What does she mean?" said James.

"All right," Shining Pearl sighed. "I'll tell you."

The boys drew closer, looking at her expectantly.

"The other reason we keep the goats isn't so pleasant," said Shining Pearl. "We use them as . . . as a sacrifice."

"I don't understand," said James. "Sacrifice to what?"

Shining Pearl took a deep breath, then let it out.

"The Goat Taker," she said.

CHAPTER 3
THE CAVE OF THE DARK WIND

"THE GOAT TAKER?" said James. "What in the world is that?"

"It's . . . a *thing* that takes goats," said Shining Pearl.

"You mean like a snake?" said Prentiss.

"No," said Shining Pearl, "it's not a snake."

"Well, what *is* it, then?" said James.

"No one knows," said Shining Pearl.

"You don't *know?*"

"Nobody has ever seen it," said Shining Pearl. "All we know is that it lives in the cave."

"The cave we're going to?" said Prentiss.

"So there's something in this cave," said James, "and it eats your goats?"

"Yes," said Shining Pearl.

"And so you *give* goats to it?"

"Yes."

"Why don't you just hunt it down?" said James. The Mollusks were superb hunters.

"We tried, once," said Shining Pearl. "But it's not so simple."

"But what . . ." began James, only to be cut off by Shining Pearl's upraised hand.

"I think it will be simpler if I just tell you what happened," she said.

"Fine," said James, impatiently. "Go ahead."

"Shoo!" said Tubby Ted to the nanny goat, who was once again displaying an interest in his trousers.

As the nanny wandered away, Shining Pearl said, "These goats have been here for many years."

"You already told us that," said Prentiss.

"I know," said Shining Pearl. "But when they first came to the island, nothing ate them, except sometimes the snakes."

"How do you know it was the snakes?" said Thomas.

"Because when a snake eats a goat, you see a big fat snake up here, with a goat-sized lump right in the middle of its body," said Shining Pearl. "And that doesn't happen often. So as I said, for a long time— *years*—nothing else was after these goats. But then there was a big storm, a terrible storm. This happened before I was born, but I've heard stories about it. The goats made it through the storm, and for the next few weeks, everything was back to normal. And then something strange happened."

"What happened?" said Prentiss.

"It was the morning after the night of a full moon. Two children—they were my great aunt and great uncle—came up to the meadow as usual to collect some goat milk," said Shining Pearl. "They noticed right away that one of the goats was missing. They knew every goat in the herd. This seemed odd to them, because the meadow is surrounded by steep hills and deep jungle; the goats *never* wander off on their own. So the children looked around, and when they got to the other side of the meadow," Shining Pearl pointed across the clearing, where the mountain rose steeply from the meadow's far edge, "they found something."

"The missing goat?" asked James.

"Not exactly," said Shining Pearl. "A trail . . . leading up the side of the mountain."

James looked around. "I don't see any trail."

"A trail of . . . blood," said Shining Pearl.

She paused, but this time the boys said nothing.

"The children ran back down to the village," she continued. "They told their father what they had seen. A group of hunters grabbed their spears and went up to the meadow. They found the . . . the trail . . . and followed it up the mountainside. It led straight into the cave."

Shining Pearl pointed to a spot about a third of the way up the mountainside above the meadow.

"It's right up there," she said.

The boys looked.

"I don't see any cave," said Thomas.

"It's hidden by the jungle," said Shining Pearl. "You can't see it unless you get close."

"So did the hunters go into the cave?" said James.

"They tried to," said Shining Pearl.

"What do you mean?" said James.

"This is not a place Mollusks like to go," said

Shining Pearl. "We are a brave people, but that cave is not a good place."

"Why not?" said James.

"The Dark Wind," said Little Scallop, breaking her silence. She shuddered.

"The WHAT?" asked Prentiss.

"It happens at night, just after sunset," said Shining Pearl.

"It blots out the moon," added Little Scallop.

"*What* does?" said James.

"Bats," said Little Scallop. She shuddered.

"Bats?" said Prentiss.

"Millions of them," said Shining Pearl.

"Millions and *millions*," added Little Scallop.

"They've lived in there forever," said Shining Pearl. "People have tried to go in there and . . . it's not a pleasant place. At night, they come out, all of them, *millions* of them, all at once. The sky around the cave is filled with bats. Their wings make the most awful sound, a roar, like a hurricane wind. That's why my people gave the cave its name." Shining Pearl said something in the Mollusk language, a mixture of grunts and clicks.

"What does that mean?" said Thomas.

"It means the 'Cave of the Dark Wind.'"

"So because of the bats, these hunters didn't go into the cave to catch whatever took the goat?" said James.

"No, they went in there," said Shining Pearl. "Or at least they tried. They got some torches, and they followed the . . . trail . . . into the cave. But things did not go well."

"What do you mean?" said James.

"Their torches went out, for one thing. The Dark Wind blew them out. Then it was *very* dark. They couldn't see a thing. The story goes that they heard noises—strange sounds, sometimes coming from ahead of them, sometimes from behind. The cavern branched into different tunnels, and branched again. Soon the hunters were lost. In the darkness, one of them fell into a pool of water—a deep pool—

and the sides were so slippery he nearly drowned before he managed to get out.

"Finally the men realized it was hopeless," she continued, "and they turned back. It took them hours to find their way out of there. One of them was lost for nearly a day, and when he finally found his way out, he was . . . blind."

"Blind?" said James.

"For a while," said Shining Pearl. "His sight came back in a few days. But he was talking like a crazy person about the things he saw in there."

"What kinds of things?" said Prentiss.

"I don't know," said Shining Pearl. "The grown-ups won't tell us. All I know is, since that day, no Mollusks have been allowed to go back into the cave."

"So you don't know what was in there that day," said James.

"No," said Shining Pearl. "But whatever it was, it's still there. A month after the first goat was taken, another one went missing. They found the same bloody trail leading to the cave, but this time nobody tried to follow it inside. They hoped it would stop, but it didn't: the next month, another goat was gone. And so it continued—always on the night of the full moon, the Goat Taker came. They tried posting guards around the meadow, but that didn't stop the Goat Taker. And in time, some members of the tribe began to worry."

"Worry about what?" said James.

"That some day, it wouldn't just take a goat," said Shining Pearl. "That some day, it would come down into the village and take one of the children." She looked down at Little Scallop and shuddered.

"And that's when they started leaving the sacrifice," continued Shining Pearl. "To keep the Goat Taker away from this meadow and as far from the village as possible. Every month, on the night of the full moon, they pick the oldest goat, lead it up the mountain and tie it outside the Cave of the Dark Wind. The next morning, it's always gone."

"A sacrifice," said Thomas.

"Yes," said Shining Pearl.

"Seems a bit cruel, doesn't it?" said Prentiss. "For the goats, I mean."

"Yes," said Shining Pearl. "It does seem cruel, and we wish we didn't have to do it. But the goats were being taken anyway, and the elders believe that the sacrifice is the best way we can protect ourselves. Since it started, the Goat Taker has never left the cave, as far as we know."

"I suppose that's something," said James.

The other boys nodded.

"So now you understand why we don't explore the cave," said Shining Pearl.

"Yes," said James. "I do understand."

"So you agree to obey the elders. To not go up there?" said Shining Pearl.

"Oh, no," said James. "Now I want to see it more than ever."

CHAPTER 4

SAVED BY THE BELL

JUST BEYOND THE SHADOWS cast by the log fort, a tall, dark figure shifted his bare feet in the shallow surf of Pirate Cove. Captain Hook's feet were rarely exposed to daylight; usually he kept them inside heavy boots the color of coal.

But today he squished his pale toes in the sand, looking for rising bubbles at the edges of incoming waves.

"Here!" Hook shouted, spotting a string of bubbles. "Dig here, Smee!"

"Aye, Cap'n!" Smee said, bustling over with a carved, hollow limb that served as a shovel. The short, round man dug quickly, following the trail of bubbles. Soon he hit a large white clam and, dropping to his knees, eagerly tore it from the wet sand with his stubby fingers. "That's number five!" he proclaimed.

"Five thus far today," sighed Hook. "Five *hundred* this month. Smee, I am sick of clams."

Puzzled, Smee looked up, the dripping clam halfway to his pocket.

"Do you want me to put it back, Cap'n?" he said.

"No, you idjit," said Hook. "I want something to eat besides clams. I'd give my right arm for . . ."

Hook stopped in midsentence, realizing that he had already given his left hand to a crocodile and could not afford to lose his right arm as well.

"What I mean," he said, "is that I would give my kingdom for a crown of beef and all the trimmings."

"Beggin' your pardon, Cap'n, but what kingdom?"

"It's an *expression*, you idjit."

The scent of rain hung in the air. Hook looked wistfully towards the horizon, tugging absentmindedly at his enormous black moustache, curled at each end.

He had once commanded a fine ship, the most

feared pirate ship on the seven seas. But he'd pursued a treasure, an elusive treasure, into a storm and had a run-in with a girl and a boy. A *flying* boy. And he'd . . . lost. He could barely stand to admit this, even to himself. Especially to himself. He'd lost not only the treasure—*for the time being*, he reminded himself—but his ship and his hand. *Everything!* An iron hook as sharp as any knife took the place of that missing hand at present. He would never be happy—truly happy—until that cursed boy was in Davy Jones's Locker, and he had a fine ship underfoot once again.

Instead of sand.

Hook wiggled his long toes, with their long, yellowed, curled nails. He spotted another trail of bubbles. "Here! Dig!"

Smee dug, and produced a sixth clam, a bit smaller than the others.

"I want some meat!" Hook whined. "I'm sick and tired of clams and coconut, coconut and clams, *clams au coconut*, coconut-battered clams, clam juice and coconut milk. SICK AND TIRED, I tell you!"

At that moment came a clatter from the jungle.

"What's that?" said Hook, turning.

From out of the jungle appeared Hurky and Boggs, two of the more enterprising of Hook's men. Hurky, a big-headed man with a flat nose, held a loop of string attached to a large nut cut open on the bottom. He shook the thing, and it clattered; it had a clapper made from a piece of hardwood.

"What have you got there?" said Hook.

"I believe it's a sort of bell, Cap'n," said Hurky.

"Really?" said Hook. "And what kind of purpose would it serve?"

Hurky answered, "Well, I was raised on a dairy farm before I went to sea, and this looks like the bells we'd hang 'round the animals' necks so we could find 'em when they wandered off."

"Is that so?" said Hook, very interested now. "And what kind of animal might that have hung from?"

Hurky picked a hair off the string and studied it. "This ain't no hair of the calf, nor bull," he said. "Nor of no pig, far as I can tell."

"Then what *is* it?" said Hook, beginning to lose patience.

"I put this to be the hair of a goat, Cap'n. We chased them scrawny things around the meadows

enough times. The devil to catch, they are, and we'd come home with this same hair on our trousers and it would scatter all over the house. Me mum used to—"

"Shut up, Hurky," said Hook.

"Aye, aye, Cap'n," said Hurky.

"Now listen," said Hook. "I want you to find that goat, you understand? You lads bring me that goat, and you'll share a fine goat-meat meal with me."

"Did you say *share*, Cap'n?" Hurky couldn't believe what he was hearing: Hook *never* shared.

"That I did."

"They get a meal, do they?" Smee muttered, as he dug another clam from under Hook's bent toes. "What about me? *I'm* the one doing all the digging."

Hook, without looking down, put his foot on the back of Smee's neck and pushed his face down into the wet sand. Smee choked and spat, drowning in one inch of water. "Do I hear someone complaining?" enquired Hook.

Smee's head shook. Water sprayed side to side.

"Good." Hook removed his foot. Smee coughed a bit, then went back to digging.

"Now, then," said Hook to Boggs and Hurky. "Where did you find this bell?"

"The other side of the island," said Boggs. "Over near them . . . you know. On a path up the hill a ways."

Hook slid the sharpened edge of the hook into the clam, prised open the shell and stirred the contents with the metal point. He then upended the shell, opened his mouth wide, and slid the oily thing down his throat in a single gulp. He burped.

"Get me that goat," he said.

"Aye, Cap'n," said Hurky and Boggs.

The two men set off into the jungle, the clatter of the wooden bell fading along with them.

CHAPTER 5

NO CHOICE

SHINING PEARL STARED AT JAMES for a moment, her mouth open in shock. When she could speak again, she said: "Are you *mad*? After what I just told you, you still want to go into the Cave of the Dark Wind?"

"I do," said James, enjoying how brave he sounded, and how scared the others looked.

"Well *I* don't," said Tubby Ted. "Not if there's bats."

"*And* a Goat Taker," added Prentiss, shivering.

"Oh, come on," said James. "Don't you at least want to *see* the cave? Isn't that better than spending another day racing snakes?"

The other boys looked doubtful, but James saw that they were at least listening, so he pressed on.

"Imagine the story we can tell Peter, when he returns," he said. "Think of the look on his face when we tell him that we saw the Cave of the Dark Wind!"

That did it for Prentiss and Thomas; like James, they were always eager to prove their courage to Peter, who was fearless.

"I don't suppose it will hurt to *look* at it," said Thomas, as Prentiss nodded. Tubby Ted was not convinced, but he usually went along with the others.

"It's settled, then," said James. "Let's go have a look."

Shining Pearl exchanged a look with Little Scallop, then said, "No. You can't go up there. It's not allowed."

"You mean *you* can't go up there," said James. "We can do what we want. We're the Lost Boys!" He turned to the other boys and said, "Let's go!" Then he started across the goat meadow, followed by Prentiss, Thomas, and, reluctantly, Tubby Ted.

Shining Pearl watched them for a moment, then shouted, "You'll get lost!"

James, not looking back, shouted, "Perhaps we will!"

Shining Pearl looked at Little Scallop. "They *will* get lost. They don't know the jungle."

"I know," said Little Scallop.

"Boys," said Shining Pearl, "can be *such* idiots."

"I know," said Little Scallop.

For a minute, the two girls stood and watched the line of four boys crossing the meadow towards the steep, thick jungle mountainside, now falling into shadow as the sun eased lower.

Finally Little Scallop said, "Should we run down to the village and tell father?"

"I thought about that," said Shining Pearl, "but by the time we get there, the boys could be lost, and we might never find them."

Little Scallop nodded.

Shining Pearl sighed and said, "I suppose we have no choice but to go with them, to keep them from killing themselves."

"I suppose so," said Little Scallop.

The two girls set off, trotting across the meadow towards the line of boys, and the dark, looming mountain jungle ahead of them.

CHAPTER 6

GOATS IN THE TREES

Determined to find their captain—and themselves—a goat for dinner, Hurky and Boggs returned to the spot where Hurky had found the wooden bell. He'd been on the eastern side of the island's steep mountain at the time, doing what the pirates spent much of their day doing, when Hook wasn't looking; he'd been sleeping.

"Right here is where I found it," said Hurky, pointing to the base of a shady tree. "Found it right here as I woke up from me nap." He stepped closer to the trunk of the tree.

"Well, there ain't no goats here now," said Boggs.

No sooner had he spoken than, from up the mountain, came the sound of bleating—*baaaaa, baaaaa*—followed by the clatter of wood.

Hurky smiled, and the two pirates began struggling up the steep incline, towards the sound of the goats. Hurky, a few yards ahead, came over a rise and found himself at the bottom of a steep mountain meadow. He looked up, and immediately turned and grabbed Boggs, dragging him down into the grass under a tree, so they would not be seen.

"*Hush!*" whispered Hurky, causing Boggs to turn his head away sharply. Hurky's breath smelled like low tide.

"What is it?" said Boggs.

"A kid!" said Hurky. "I seen a big kid up there."

"Well of *course* you did," said Boggs. "It's *goats*, isn't it?"

"Not a *goat* kid," whispered Hurky. "It's a *human* kid I seen."

"Ah," said Boggs.

Cautiously, the two pirates raised their heads and peeked over the grass. The meadow was steeply pitched. At the upper end, they counted not one, but two . . . three . . . *six* children, heading for the steep jungle hillside that rose over the meadow.

"It's them boys," said Hurky. "And two island girls."

"Where are the goats?" Boggs asked.

Again, as if in answer, came the sound—*baaaaa*. It came from . . . directly over their heads.

Hurky and Boggs looked up.

Goats. Three of them. Standing calmly in the branches of the tree.

Hurky and Boggs looked at each other and then around the meadow. They saw more goats, dozens of them, including quite a few in trees, their hooves delicately placed on branches as they craned their necks to nibble the leaves.

"This is a very strange island," said Boggs.

"That it is," said Hurky, shaking his head.

"So," said Boggs, "let's catch one for dinner."

Hurky frowned, thinking. "Not just yet," he said.

"Why not?" said Boggs.

"We can come back for the goats," Hurky said. "They ain't going nowhere."

"But the cap'n—" began Boggs.

"The cap'n," interrupted Hurky, "is always very interested in them boys. And I think them boys is up to something, straying this far from the native camp. I say we follow 'em up that hillside and see what they's up to. That way, we bring the cap'n his goat *and* some word on them boys. I bet he gives us extra goat as a reward."

Boggs smiled, liking the sound of that.

"All right," he said. "Let's follow them boys."

CHAPTER 7

SUPERSTITION

J AMES AND PRENTISS LED THE WAY, shoving aside
leaves as big as themselves, following what might
have been a trail, but in any case was the only way
they could find through the thick jungle. They
ducked beneath giant spiderwebs that looked more
like fishing nets and avoided holes in the soft earth
that might be the homes of the wrong kinds of
snakes. Thomas and Tubby Ted struggled behind,
constantly calling out for the other two to wait.

But James was in no mood to wait for anyone. He
wanted to see the mysterious cave.

After struggling up the hillside for what seemed

like an hour, the boys came to a clearing. It looked as if a giant had taken a bite out of the hillside. In front of them was a wall of rough rock, and in the middle of the wall was a thick curtain of twisting vines.

Cautiously, James stepped forward and pushed some vines aside. To his surprise, they parted easily. He looked inside.

Darkness.

Not dark rock, but just plain dark, as if he had opened the door to a cellar. James stuck his head in. He peered into the darkness, but could see nothing. He felt cool, damp air on his face and felt a chill through his body—and not just because of the cool air. He pulled his head back out and looked at the others.

"This is it," he said. "The cave."

One by one, the other boys poked their heads through the vine curtain, looked at the darkness, then pulled their heads back out.

"It's very dark," said Prentiss.

"It smells funny," said Tubby Ted.

"Maybe we shouldn't go in there," said Thomas. "Maybe Shining Pearl was right."

Before James could answer, a voice came from behind them, making all four boys jump.

"I'm glad *one* of you has some sense," said Shining Pearl. She stepped out of the jungle, followed by Little Scallop.

"I thought you were going back," said James.

"Someone has to look after you," said Shining Pearl.

"We don't need looking after," said James, although, in fact, he felt relieved to see Shining Pearl.

"If you're going in there," she said, pointing to the vines, "you most certainly *do* need looking after."

Prentiss, Thomas, and Tubby Ted all looked at James, waiting to hear what he had to say to that. James felt them staring at him. He looked at Shining Pearl.

"We're going in," he said, crossing his arms to show he meant it.

"B . . . but what about the Goat Taker?" said Thomas, looking at the vines.

"That's just a superstition," said James.

"What's a super . . . a super stitching?" said Thomas.

"It's when people believe something that's not real," said James. He looked at Shining Pearl and added, "Somebody tells a silly story, and people come to believe it."

"It's not a story," said Shining Pearl. "The goats were gone. The blood was there. And *something* made one of the warriors go blind."

All eyes were on James again. It was as if he could feel the stares burning into his skin.

"Well, we're not afraid," he said. He looked at the other three boys. "Are we?"

"No," said Prentiss, though he was.

Thomas, who was too scared to speak, nodded.

"I could stay out here with the girls and make sure they don't go and tell anyone," volunteered Tubby Ted.

"No," said James. "We all go in together. Come on."

He stepped through the vines. Someone—something—passed through here regularly. James didn't mention this to the others. He stuck his head back outside.

"Come on," he repeated. "It's just a dumb old story."

Prentiss stepped forward, followed by Thomas, and then—very reluctantly—Tubby Ted.

Much relieved, James turned, and the others followed him into the Cave of the Dark Wind.

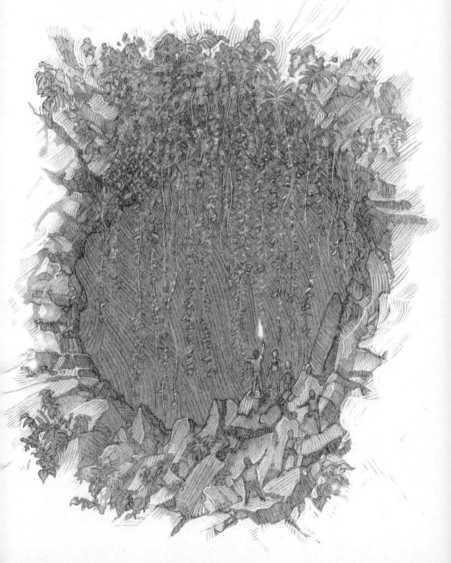

CHAPTER 8

A STRANGE SOUND

For THE FIRST FEW STEPS, there was enough light coming through the vines for the boys to see where they were going. Ahead of them the cave went straight into the mountain, disappearing into blackness, with no end in sight.

Like a giant throat, thought James. *And it's swallowing us.*

He wanted to turn right around and leave, but he felt he couldn't—not after making such a fuss about wanting to go inside. So he went forward cautiously, grateful for the sound of shuffling footsteps telling him that the other boys were following behind him.

Deeper and deeper into the cave they went, until they were all in total blackness. James stopped, and Prentiss bumped into him. Then Thomas bumped into Prentiss, and Tubby Ted into Thomas.

"Are we going to turn around?" asked Thomas. He spoke in a near whisper, but his voice sounded surprisingly loud in the dark stillness of the cave. James was about to agree that they should turn back. But then, peering ahead, he saw a dim light.

"We'll go a little farther," he whispered, feeling his way forward with his feet. The source of the light was a hole in the cave roof—a lava tube, no thicker than an arm, twisting and turning its way to the surface far above. James studied it, then shuffled forward. Soon they were in near total darkness again, but a few steps on, James saw the wan glow of another lava tube. They passed through several more alternating patches of blackness and dim light, the air around them growing cooler and damper. After a while, the lava tubes grew fewer, and though the boys' eyes had adjusted to the darkness, they could see nothing. Their bare feet were now walking on something oozy and squishy. James hoped it was mud, but it didn't smell like mud. It made the boys' toes curl trying not to touch it too much.

"James?" whispered Thomas. "Isn't this far enough?"

"There are bound to be more of those light holes up ahead," whispered James.

"But what if there aren't?" said Prentiss.

"Then we'll turn around and come back with torches."

"But when the Mollusks used torches," Tubby Ted said, remembering the story, "the Dark Wind blew them out." He shuddered, thinking about the bats, wondering if they were hanging over his head right now, somewhere in the blackness above him.

"Just a little farther," said James.

He started to inch forward.

"UNNH!"

James's grunt of pain echoed loudly in the blackness, followed by the smack of his hands hitting the cave floor.

"What happened?" said Thomas.

"Are you all right?" said Prentiss.

"Yes," said James, scrambling to his feet. "I tripped on something. It's—"

He stopped in midsentence, cut off by a strange

sound. It came from somewhere ahead, deeper in the cave. It echoed through the damp blackness—a mournful, moaning sound.

Singing.

The boys couldn't make out the words, but the tune was familiar to them. They'd heard sailors sing it on the *Never Land*. It was a sad, slow shanty about a ship lost at sea.

But who was singing it now?

Tubby Ted whispered what they all were thinking: "The Goat Taker."

The boys turned and ran.

In a few steps Tubby Ted fell; the other three tripped and fell on top of him. They scrambled to their feet and resumed running blindly. They came to a lava hole and, able to see a bit, ran even faster. Then it got dark, and they tripped again but popped up immediately and continued running. They continued their madhouse up-and-down race until they finally saw green ahead and burst through the curtain of vines and into the fresh air, where they dropped to their hands and knees, gasping for breath.

Shining Pearl and Little Scallop stood waiting for

them. Shining Pearl had an I-told-you-so smile on her face.

"So," she said, looking right at James. "It's just a dumb old story, is it?"

James ignored her.

"I found something!" he gasped. "I tripped on it back there and picked it up!"

"What is it?" said Thomas.

James reached between his knees, pulled out the thing he'd carried from the cave . . . and instantly dropped it. He jumped away from it, as did Thomas and Tubby Ted.

Shining Pearl gasped; Prentiss and Little Scallop screamed.

James had carried out a human skull.

CHAPTER 9

THE WINKING SKULL

THE TWO GIRLS AND FOUR BOYS stared down at the skull. It grinned back up at them with chipped and blackened teeth.

"I thought it was a bowl," whispered James, mostly to himself. "Or a coconut."

"That's no coconut," said Tubby Ted.

"I think we should go now," said Prentiss.

"Wait a minute," said Little Scallop. "What are those . . . those shiny things in its eyes?"

James knelt and peered at the skull.

"They're coins!" he said.

Sure enough, above the skull's broken teeth and

the jagged hole where a nose had once been, sat two thick coins. They stared at the children like unblinking eyes.

"They're *gold* coins," whispered James.

"But whose *head* is it?" said Prentiss.

"Maybe," said James, "it's the Goat Taker's head. Maybe he died a long time ago."

"Then who put the coins in his eyes?" said Shining Pearl.

James had no answer for that, but he had another question. "What if there are more coins?" he said. "What if there's a real treasure in that cave?" James thought about how impressed Peter would be if he told him that he had found a real treasure.

"Whatever it is," said Shining Pearl, "we need to show it to my father."

Her father was Fighting Prawn, chief of the Mollusks. He was a good man who protected the boys from the pirates. But James knew that Fighting Prawn would not want the boys going back into the cave. And the more James thought about it, the more he wanted to find the treasure, so he could brag about it to Peter.

"If you tell your father," he said to Shining Pearl, "he won't let us go back in there."

"Exactly," she answered.

"But if we go back in there," he said, "we might find a treasure."

"I don't care," she said.

"That's not all we might find," said James.

"What do you mean?"

"We might solve the mystery of the Goat Taker," said James. "Think how many goats that would save! Think how happy that would make your tribe."

Shining Pearl hesitated. It *would* be wonderful to stop the goat sacrifices. And she would love to impress her father, the way her big brothers were always doing.

"Well," she said. "I suppose if we were very careful . . ."

"Of course we'll be careful," said James.

"B . . . but what about the skull?" said Thomas.

"It's old," said James. "Probably pirates hid the treasure here long ago, and they left the skull here to scare people away."

"Well it worked," said Prentiss, " 'cause I'm scared."

"But whoever hid it is gone, don't you see?" said James.

"Then who was singing?" said Tubby Ted.

"We don't *know* who was singing," said James. "It's the cave of the Dark Wind, right? Maybe it was the wind. Or the bats. Or maybe just an echo. Maybe we were hearing ourselves."

"But we weren't singing," said Thomas.

Instead of arguing, James picked up the skull and prised a gold coin out of one of the eye sockets. He held it up, so the late-day sun glinted off its shiny surface. Everyone stared at the coin.

"Treasure," said James. "Gold treasure. We could find a gold treasure and solve the Goat Taker mystery!"

"Or go blind," reminded Shining Pearl.

"But we *didn't*," said James. "We went in there, and we came out, and nothing happened. Tomorrow we'll come back with torches. We'll be fine, you'll see. Don't you want to save your goats?"

Shining Pearl looked worried. "Of course I do," she said. "But we don't know what's in there. We don't know. . . ."

Her voice trailed off as she looked down at the

skull with a gold coin in one eye socket and the other socket empty. The skull seemed to be winking at her. She looked at James.

"Promise you'll be careful," she said.

James smiled at her. "I promise," he said.

CHAPTER 10

DARKNESS

Boggs and Hurky saw it all from behind a large rubber plant at the edge of the clearing.

They saw the four boys go into the cave, saw the two girls waiting for them, saw the boys come stumbling back out of the cave, terrified.

They saw the skull.

And then they saw the gold.

At the sight of the yellow coin glinting in James's hand, Boggs grabbed Hurky's arm and squeezed it so hard that Hurky almost cried out.

"That there's a gold doubloon," Boggs whispered. Hurky, his eyes nearly as large as the boy's gold coin, nodded furiously.

Boggs and Hurky were not the smartest crewmen, but they knew the meaning of gold coins in a skull's eyes. It was a message as old as pirates themselves: BEWARE.

"That there skull was left by a pirate," whispered Boggs. "A pirate trying to protect his treasure."

"Aye," said Hurky, staring hungrily at the gold coin in the boy's hand, glinting in the sun.

"Cap'n will want to hear about this," said Boggs. "Come on!"

Quietly, the two men melted into the jungle. They made their way down to Goat Meadow and found the trail that would take them back to the pirate side of the island. They broke into a trot, eager to get to the fort and tell Captain Hook the news.

After a few minutes of running, they reached a clearing. They paused to catch their breath. Hurky looked up at the big mountain that divided the island. He frowned and rubbed his eyes.

Boggs blinked a couple of times. The sun wasn't down yet, but suddenly the clearing seemed darker. He glanced up, expecting to see clouds.

But there were no clouds. The sun was low, but still a few minutes from setting.

"Hurky," said Boggs, rubbing his eyes.

"I'm over here," said Hurky, still looking towards the mountain, blinking furiously. "There's something wrong with my eyes, I think."

"Me too," said Boggs, rubbing furiously. "Like it's night falling. But it ain't night yet."

"I can't see the mountain no more!" said Hurky, his voice fearful.

Then, slowly, as if an enormous shade were being lowered, the world turned to darkness for Hurky and Boggs.

"Hurky!" said Boggs, blinking furiously, "I can't see nothing!"

"Me neither!" said Hurky. "It's like I've gone . . ."

"Blind," said Boggs.

CHAPTER 11

THE ROAR OF WAVES

THE SUN, ALMOST GONE NOW, was just a half circle peeking over the horizon, and getting smaller by the second. The children were eager to get back to their huts, away from the cave. They started down the mountainside towards Goat Meadow, with Shining Pearl leading the way. She was followed by Little Scallop, then James, who held the skull, and the other three boys. They had gone only a few steps when the sun dipped below the horizon.

And then they heard the sound.

It came from behind them, from the cave. The children froze in their footsteps and turned. They looked up at the mouth of the cave, visible in the twilight on the mountainside rising behind them.

The sound came again. To James, it sounded like the roar of waves crashing on a beach. But it came from inside the cave. And it was getting louder. Closer.

"Wh— what *is* that?" said Prentiss. "Is that the Goat Taker?"

"No," said Shining Pearl, "that's the Dark Wind."

"Should we run away?" asked Thomas.

"You can't run away," said Little Scallop. "It goes too fast."

The sound was getting louder.

"So what do we do?" said James.

"Get under the trees," Shining Pearl said urgently. "And stay down."

The children ran off the path and crouched beneath a clump of trees. They peered through the branches at the cave mouth. The twilight deepened; stars appeared in the darkening sky, and the roaring sound grew louder, and still louder.

"Look!" shouted Prentiss, pointing.

A small black shape shot from the cave, swooping and darting. It was followed by another, and another. . . .

Dozens.

Then hundreds.

Then thousands.

Then millions.

Now the roaring sound was upon them, and the sky overhead was blotted out completely, filled with bats. The trees shook from the wind created by the furiously fluttering wings. Thomas was shouting something to James, but the noise of the bats was so loud James couldn't hear what it was.

On and on it went, the bats sweeping over the huddling children in a dark rushing tide that seemed to have no end. The boys watched with gaping mouths, each thinking the same thing: they had been inside the cave, in the dark, *with all those bats*.

Finally, after the longest time, the roar started to taper off, and the river of flying shapes thinned out. It was fully dark now; the children could see stars again as the last of the bats flitted past.

The night was silent; even the insects were quiet.

"So," said Shining Pearl, looking at James, "do you still want to go back into the cave?"

James looked at her, then at the other boys, all watching him anxiously. He looked down at the skull still clutched in his right hand. With his left hand he held up the coin he'd removed from the eye socket. It glinted in the starlight. He thought about the bats and the gold. Then he thought about Peter.

Then he looked back at Shining Pearl.

"They're only bats," he said. "Although I'll grant you, there are quite a few."

"Quite a few?" said Shining Pearl. "Quite a *few*?"

"They'll be sound asleep in the morning," said James, "when we go back into that cave."

CHAPTER 12

BLIND LUCK

CAPTAIN HOOK WAS NOT HAPPY.

"Smee!" he roared.

"Aye, Cap'n!" said Smee, coming through the doorway. "I'm right—OOOF."

Smee tripped over the door frame, as he did every time he entered Hook's hut. He landed facedown, the top of his head two inches from the tips of Hook's black boots.

"Aye, Cap'n," he said, to the floor.

"Smee," said Hook, "you are an idjit."

"Aye, Cap'n," said Smee, getting up. "Will there be anything else?"

"YES, THERE WILL BE SOMETHING ELSE," roared Hook. "Do you think I called you in here just to watch you fall down?"

"No, Cap'n," said Smee, although there had been days when Hook was so bored that he did, in fact, call Smee into his hut just to watch him fall down.

"I'm hungry, Smee," said Hook. "I want my dinner."

"Aye, Cap'n," said Smee. "Cook made a nice lizard stew that I could . . ."

"I DON'T WANT LIZARD STEW!" roared Hook. "I want GOAT. WHERE'S MY GOAT, SMEE?"

"Your goat ain't here, Cap'n," said Smee, ducking his head in case Hook decided to hit him.

"Not here?" said Hook. "Why not?"

"Boggs and Hurky ain't returned, Cap'n," said Smee.

Hook looked out the doorway. Night had fallen. The pirates hated to be outside the fort after dark, when deadly creatures roamed the jungle. If Boggs and Hurky had not returned, they must be in trouble. And that worried Hook. Because if his men were in trouble, he might not get his goat dinner.

"Smee," he said, "send a search party out for Boggs and Hurky."

"Now?" said Smee.

"No," said Hook. "Next Christmas."

"Aye, aye, Cap'n," said Smee. "But we ain't got a calendar, so how will I . . ."

"I DON'T WANT YOU TO SEND 'EM OUT NEXT CHRISTMAS, YOU IDJIT," bellowed Hook. "I WANT YOU TO SEND 'EM OUT NOW."

"Aye, aye, Cap'n," said Smee, scurrying off, wondering what Christmas had to do with it. He tripped over the door frame on his way out.

It was three hours before the search party returned. By then Hook was a very unhappy captain indeed. He'd become so hungry waiting for his goat dinner, that he'd eaten some lizard stew, which tasted like . . . well, like stewed lizard.

So he was in a bad, bad mood when he heard the search party return to the fort. He stomped out of his hut and found the searchers, still holding torches, in a semicircle around Boggs and Hurky, who knelt on the ground, their faces, arms, and legs covered with scratches and insect bites.

"What took you so long?" Hook said. "And where's my goat?"

"Cap'n," whimpered Boggs. "We can't see."

"What do you mean, you can't see?" said Hook.

"We've gone blind," said Hurky. "All at once. It was like the sun went down, only it wasn't down."

"We found 'em over the other side of the mountain," said one of the searchers. "They was shouting and crying like babies."

"No we wasn't," said Hurky.

"Yes you was," said the searcher.

"Not like *babies*, we wasn't," said Boggs.

"QUIET, YOU IDJITS!" said Hook. "Hurky, tell me what happened, and it better be good."

"Aye, Cap'n," said Hurky. "We went over to where the goats was, like you told us. But then we seen them boys."

"Did you see the *flying* boy?" interrupted Hook, always interested in catching Peter.

"No, Cap'n," said Hurky. "But we seen the other four, with two of them island girls. We followed 'em to a cave."

"A cave," said Hook, getting more interested. "Go on."

"They argued about going in," said Hurky. "We couldn't hear it too good, but the girls said there was something bad in the cave. But the boys went in anyway. About ten minutes later they come running out, scared half to death. And one of 'em was holding a skull."

He had Hook's full attention now.

"A human skull?" said Hook.

"Aye, Cap'n. With a gold doubloon in each eye."

There were gasps from the men. *Gold.*

Hook frowned. "Did you get a good look at the coins?" he said. "Both of you?"

Boggs and Hurky nodded.

"And how long after that did you go blind?" said Hook.

"Right then," answered Hurky. "Took only a minute."

Hook did something then that surprised his men, at least those who could see him.

He smiled.

"The Blind Luck Treasure," he said.

More gasps from the men.

"Begging the cap'n's pardon, Cap'n," said Smee. "But what's that?"

"The Blind Luck Treasure," said Hook, a dreamy look crossing his face, "was a great treasure taken by the Spaniards. Gold it was, found in a mine deep in the high mountains of Peru. The natives warned the Spaniards not to take the gold. They said it was sacred, and if anybody took it, the gold would become cursed, and those who took it would suffer for their greed. But the Spaniards didn't listen. They minted the gold into doubloons right there at the mine, and they filled chest after chest with those doubloons, a dozen chests and more. Then they put those chests on a ship called the *Mariposa*. She set sail for Spain, but she soon ran into trouble."

"Did pirates get her?" said Smee.

"No," said Hook. "The crew started going blind."

Everyone looked at Hurky and Boggs.

"It turned out that the natives were telling the

truth," continued Hook. "The treasure *was* cursed. Once at sea, the crew of the *Mariposa* hauled a trunk on deck, to have a look at the gold. Some looked at it for a few minutes; some for hours. One by one they lost their sight. How long they lost it depended on how long they looked. Some could see again in a few hours; some never did. There was only one aboard who wasn't affected."

"Who was that?" said Smee.

"The cabin boy, a young lad the crew called No Beard. He could look at the gold all he wanted. In time they figured out that, being just a boy, he felt no greed for the gold, so the curse left him alone. For a time he was the only one in the crew who could see. He had to steer the ship, with the men handling the lines and sails by feel."

"Is that how they made it to Spain?" said Smee.

"They never made it to Spain," said Hook. "The sailors who got their sight back wanted off that ship, away from the cursed treasure. Soon as they could see, they lowered the two longboats and rowed away, leaving No Beard steering a ship crewed by blind men. Only one of those longboats made it to land to tell the story . . . or part of the story, anyway."

"What do you mean, Cap'n?" said Smee.

"A month later," said Hook, "a British navy ship picked up some men floating in the sea near an island, holding on to some barrels. The men were blind; they were sailors from the *Mariposa*. They said the ship got caught in a storm and started to break apart; they were washed overboard. The navy ship searched for days—the sea and the island—but found no trace of the *Mariposa*, or No Beard, or any of the other crew. Or the gold. Many men have looked for that gold since; it came to be known as the Blind Luck Treasure. I've searched for it myself, a time or two, with no luck."

Hook licked his lips.

"And now it's here," he said. "Right here, on *this* island."

"But Cap'n," said Smee. "It's cursed."

Hook spat on the ground.

"Curse or no," he said. "It's gold."

The group was silent for a moment, every man thinking about the gold. The silence was broken by Boggs, still kneeling.

"I can see!" he cried. He was looking at one of the torches, tears streaming down his face. "I can see the light! Me sight is coming back!"

"So's mine!" exclaimed Hurky, blinking.

Hook looked at the two kneeling men, his smile revealing a mouth half-full of brown and crooked teeth.

"Good," he said softly. "Now you can lead us to that cave."

CHAPTER 13

THE SIGHTLESS CATERPILLAR

JAMES PULLED THE VINES ASIDE and shoved the smoking torch through the gap. "Here we go," he said.

Tubby Ted, Prentiss, and Thomas hesitated.

"Come on!" said James. "This torch won't last forever."

That was surely true. James had made the torch from dry grass soaked in fish oil and wrapped it with vines. Half of it had burned away during the climb from the boys' hut to the cave.

James stepped through the vine curtain. Reluctantly, the other three boys followed him. By the torch's flickering light, the boys could see what they had not seen the day before: the cave entrance led to a narrow passage lined with black lava rock. In a few yards it opened to a large, high chamber. The boys' eyes were drawn upwards.

"Look!" said Thomas, pointing. "The ceiling is moving."

Sure enough, the black ceiling was rippling in a wavelike motion. A rustling sound echoed through the vast room.

"Bats," whispered Prentiss. "The whole ceiling is *bats*."

"I'm going," said Tubby Ted. He turned to leave but could see only a few feet ahead of him by the dwindling light of the torch. Beyond that was blackness.

"Which way is out?" he said.

James ignored him. He was looking at the floor, which was covered with a gooey, squishy gray paste. In it were footprints. Some were fresh, clearly made the day before by the boys' bare feet. But there were other, older prints as well. Some looked like animal prints. A *goat's*, thought James. But there were some other prints as well. Larger ones.

Human ones.

Who made those? James wondered. He almost wondered it out loud but decided that the other three boys were scared enough already. They crowded close to him and the torch, staring up at the rippling, rustling ceiling of bats.

Then the torch sputtered.

Then it went out.

The cave went black, blacker than the blackest night.

"I think we should leave now," said Prentiss.

"I think we never should have come in," said Thomas.

"But which way is out?" said Tubby Ted, his voice rising in fear.

Overhead, the rustling grew louder.

"Quiet!" whispered James. "You're disturbing the bats."

"Not as much as they're disturbing *me*," said Tubby Ted.

"If we just wait a minute," said James, "our eyes will get used to the dark."

They waited, and in a few minutes, as James had promised, they saw a soft glow well in front of them—light spilling through a lava tube.

"We'll go towards the light," said James.

"But that's deeper into the cave," said Tubby Ted. "At least, I think it is."

"You want to go back alone?" said James, moving towards the light.

"Wait! I'm coming!" said Tubby Ted.

The four boys shuffled slowly towards the light. James walked with his hands out in front of him, feeling his way through the empty, black space. The other three crowded close behind. James sensed that they had entered a narrower space, and he reached out sideways. On both sides he touched rough, cold rock.

"It's a tunnel," he announced. "Stay behind me."

The others followed him into the tunnel, too scared to talk.

As it turned out, the light from the lava tube came down in the middle of this tunnel. James looked to the floor and saw that the goat prints— and the footprints—continued through here. Saying nothing, he moved ahead, the other boys following.

They passed under several more lava tubes, then left the tunnel and entered what felt like another large space. The air was suddenly colder, and the darkness was again complete. James couldn't see his hands in front of him. He stopped. Prentiss bumped into him, then Thomas into Prentiss, then Tubby Ted into Thomas. Thirty seconds passed in total silence.

"What are we waiting for?" whispered Thomas.

"Quiet," said James. The truth is, he was waiting for his eyes to pick up some light, somewhere. But the longer he waited, the darker the cave seemed to be. He was beginning to think the others were right—maybe it was time to turn back. But it was so dark that James didn't know if he could find the way.

"I'm scared," whispered Prentiss, speaking for all of them.

"We'll be all right," said James.

"But we can't *see* anything," said Prentiss.

"I think this was a mistake," said Thomas.

"I agree," said a new voice, from behind the boys.

All four boys jumped. Tubby Ted fell down. Prentiss and Thomas yelped. James whirled towards the sound of the voice and said, in a voice that sounded braver than he felt, "WHO'S THERE?"

"It's me," said the voice. "Shining Pearl."

"What are *you* doing here?" said James.

"Rescuing a bunch of lost boys," said Shining Pearl.

"We're not lost!" snapped James.

"Really?" said Shining Pearl. "Then where are you?"

The cave was silent for a moment.

"Okay," said James. "Maybe we're a little lost. But we're not leaving until we find the treasure."

Shining Pearl sighed. "I knew you'd say that. I guess if I can't get you to leave, I can at least lead you to your stupid treasure, so you don't starve to death in here."

"I don't see how you can help us," said James. "Can you see in the dark?"

"No," said Shining Pearl. "But I can find my way around. For example, I can smell the fresh water ahead. Can you?"

The air was filled with the sound of four boys sniffing.

After a long pause, James said, "Okay, you've made your point. Now what?"

"Now," said Shining Pearl, "you follow me." She moved in front of the boys. "Take hold of my waist," she told James. "You others form a line behind James and take hold of each other's waists."

The boys did as they were told. When they were all connected, Shining Pearl said, "Let's go."

And so, like a sightless caterpillar, they moved deeper into the cave.

CHAPTER 14

NOTHING TO FEAR

OUTSIDE THE CAVE ENTRANCE, Hook emerged from the jungle, followed by Smee and eight pirates, including Boggs and Hurky, who by now could see normally again. Though it was bright daylight, two of the men carried burning torches.

They gathered in front of the cave mouth, where Hook gave his orders.

"You men will go in first," he said, pointing to the torchbearers. "Keep your eyes open, but if you see any gold, don't look at it."

"Begging the cap'n's pardon," said Smee, "but if they see the gold, how are they going to not look at it?"

"I'm glad you asked that question, Smee," said

Hook, with a glare that said he was not glad at all.

"Aye, Cap'n" said Smee. "I asked because when Hurky and Boggs . . ."

"Shut up, Smee," said Hook.

"Aye, Cap'n."

"What I mean is, these men can safely look at the gold for a *moment*," said Hook, who had no idea whether this was true. "Once they find the gold, we'll cover it up before we carry it out."

"How will we cover it up if we can't look at it?" asked Smee.

"We'll use this," said Hook, drawing a knife. Its blade, polished to a mirrorlike finish, gleamed in the sun.

"We're going to stab the gold?" said Smee.

"No, you idjit," said Hook. "We'll look at the *reflection* of the gold in the knife blade. That way the gold can't hurt us." Hook had no idea whether this was true, either, but it seemed to satisfy the men.

"All right," said Hook. "Into the cave."

The two torchbearers parted the vine curtain and stepped into the cave, followed by Hook, Smee, and the others. They moved forward slowly, pausing every few steps to look at their surroundings. When they reached the first large chamber, Hook ordered everyone to halt. He studied the cave floor, which was covered with footprints of various types and sizes.

"These here," he said, pointing to some prints of smallish bare feet, "are the boys. Looks like they were in here more than once." He frowned. "And seeing as how these prints here ain't made the return trip, looks as if the boys are in here now, ahead of us somewhere."

Hook pointed at some other, older prints. "Now these here," he said, "belong to a man."

"One of the islanders?" said Smee, a note of fear in his voice. The pirates did not get along well with the Mollusk tribe.

"Maybe," said Hook, looking ahead at the blackness beyond the torchlight. "But whoever it is, there's only one of him. There's ten of us. We've nothing to fear! Forward, men. Let's find that gold!"

Despite his brave words, Hook was concerned about the larger footprints. He wondered who had made them. And he wondered if that person was waiting for them in the darkness ahead.

And so, just in case, Hook made sure he was walking several steps behind the torchbearers as the pirates made their way deeper into the cave.

CHAPTER 15

THE VOICE IN THE DARK

THE HUMAN CATERPILLAR, with Shining Pearl leading and the four boys following behind her, twisted slowly through the cold darkness, then stopped. By the dim glow of an overhead lava tube, the children saw that the cave once again branched off into two tunnels. They could see only a few feet into each tunnel, beyond which lay blackness. There was no sound but the *drip-drip-drip* of water falling from the cave roof, and their own breathing.

This was the fourth time they'd had to choose between two tunnels. Each time, they'd waited for Shining Pearl's nose to decide.

She sniffed the air, then pointed to the right-hand tunnel.

"That way," she said. She moved forward, followed by the boys, each holding the waist of the person ahead. James, who was right behind Shining Pearl, tried to remember the turns they'd made so far, but he was getting confused. Was it *left, right, left, right?* Or *right, left, left, right?*

James realized that he was quite lost. But Shining Pearl seemed sure of herself, as if she just *knew* which way to go. And as far as James could tell, she was right: anytime a lava tube offered enough light for him to see the cave floor, there were goat tracks at their feet.

Sometimes there were also bones. Goat bones, James hoped, but didn't dare check. And sometimes the goo underfoot became as thick as batter, rising over their ankles and smelling something awful. But so far, there was no sign of gold.

The caterpillar moved forward slowly, its ten feet shuffling on the cold, wet cave floor. Suddenly Shining Pearl stopped again. The four boys bumped into one another.

"What is it?" whispered James.

"I thought I heard . . . " said Shining Pearl.

"What?" whispered Thomas.

"Singing," said James. "I hear it, too."

All five were listening now, straining to hear the sounds drifting to them from the cold blackness ahead.

"That's not the wind," said Shining Pearl.

"No," said James. "That's a voice . . . a man's voice."

The voice sang in a high, wavering pitch. James couldn't make out the words, but he recognized the tune as the same sea shanty he and the others had heard the day before. And whoever was singing it was not far off. Not far at all.

"I think we should leave," said Tubby Ted, from the back of the caterpillar.

"Me too," said Prentiss.

"Shhh," said Shining Pearl. "I hear something else."

They listened again, and the boys heard it.

Clink-clink-clink.

"What's that?" said Thomas.

"It's metal," said Shining Pearl.

"It's gold," said James.

"You don't know that," said Shining Pearl.

"But it *could* be," said James.

"It could be an axe," said Prentiss. "Or a knife."

"I'm leaving," said Tubby Ted.

"Me too," said Prentiss.

"No! You'll get lost," said Shining Pearl. "You don't know the way out."

"I'll take my chances."

"But we made several turns," said James. "You could get *really* lost. You'd better stay with us."

"And get chopped to pieces by an axe?" said Ted. "No, thank you. Good-bye."

"Wait for me!" said Prentiss. "I'm going with you."

With that, Tubby Ted and Prentiss let go of the caterpillar and turned back. The sound of their shuffling feet grew fainter, then it was gone.

The remaining three children—Shining Pearl, James, and Thomas—all thought about going with them. But nobody wanted to be the one to sound scared. And so—though they all *were* scared—they started forward again.

The singing grew louder with every step. So did the *clink-clink-clink*.

"Gold," whispered James, mostly to reassure himself.

"We must be getting closer," said Thomas.

"Yes," said Shining Pearl. "But to *what?*"

CHAPTER 16

THE WARNING

THE PIRATES WERE BURNING their second pair of torches. They had used the dying flames from the first pair to light the second; they had one pair left. As they moved deeper and deeper into the cave, some of the men began to wonder if they would have enough light to find their way back out. But they didn't dare voice their fears to Hook.

Hook was third in line, right behind the two torchbearers, his glittering dark eyes scouring the cave floor for footprints. They had followed the children's prints through a series of tunnel branches, sometimes turning right, sometimes left. Hook wondered how the children knew which way to go. With each turn, he became more convinced that the children weren't wandering aimlessly—that they had a destination in mind.

They know where it is, he told himself. *They're heading for the treasure.*

"Cap'n!" shouted one of the torchbearers, halting suddenly.

"What is it?" said Hook, straining to see ahead in the reflection of his knife blade. He was determined not to be among those who went blind, but he wasn't very good with using the knife as a mirror. He gasped when, by the dancing light of the torch flames, he saw it: a human skeleton. Not seeing any gold, he turned and looked without the knife. It was propped in a sitting position against the cave wall, its arms out to the sides, its legs spread apart. It was about ten feet away, off to the side of the path they were following. Hook glanced down: the footprints indicated that the children had passed right by the skeleton without stopping—had they not seen it?

Hook looked more closely at the skeleton. The skull seemed to be looking back at him with a crooked grin, as if it found the situation amusing.

Around the skeleton's neck was a rope, and hanging from that rope was a rough wooden board with something written on it.

"Put some light on that board," Hook barked to the torchbearers.

Reluctantly, the two men edged towards the skeleton.

"Cap'n," said one of the men. "It's holding something in its hands!"

Hook once again raised his knife as a precaution and angled its gleaming blade to look down. There he saw that both of the skeleton's bony hands resting on the cave floor held an object that twinkled with reflected torchlight. As he strained to make out the objects, he noticed—

"LOOK AWAY!" he shouted. "DON'T LOOK AT IT!" Quickly, the others turned away from the skeleton.

"What is it, Cap'n?" asked Smee.

"The Blind Luck Treasure," said Hook, still using the knife.

"The whole treasure?" said Smee.

"No," said Hook. "Just two doubloons, one in each of the skeleton's hands." He felt a little sting to

his eyes, and wondered if maybe he could go blind even using the knife.

"Where's the rest of it?" said Smee.

"I don't know," said Hook, rubbing his eyes. "But there's a sign around the skeleton's neck that might tell us." Not taking any chances, he passed his knife to Smee. "Read the sign. Hold my knife . . . right like this."

"Me?"

"You."

Smee did as he was told. "Hmm," he said.

"What's the matter?" Hook asked.

"It seems to be a foreign language," said Smee. "Definitely not English. It starts out KCABOG. Wait a minute! The letters aren't right."

"What do you mean, they aren't right?" said Hook.

"They look backwards."

"THEY ARE BACKWARDS, YOU IDJIT!" said Hook.

"But why would anybody write a sign backwards?" said Smee. "Some kind of code, d'you think?"

Hook took a deep breath, then exhaled.

"Smee," Hook said, forcing himself to sound

calm. "Just read me the letters. Boggs, you write the letters in the dirt on the floor with your finger."

"Aye, aye, Cap'n," said Smee, squinting. "K C A B O G is the first line. The second line is R O. The third one says "D N I L B O G. That's the lot, Cap'n."

Hook went over to where Boggs had written the letters on the floor. They looked like this:

K C A B O G

R O

D N I L B O G

Hook squatted and, using his hook, scrawled the letters on the cave floor in reverse order, adding two spaces. The men gathered around, staring at the words:

GO BACK

OR

GO BLIND

It was Smee who finally broke the silence.

"So we'll be turning back now, Cap'n?" he said.

"Turn back?" said Hook. "Turn *back*, when there's a fortune in gold ahead of us? Enough to make every man here *rich*?"

"Rich and blind," muttered a voice.

"WHO SAID THAT?" shouted Hook, glaring at the pirates. Nobody answered.

"We're going ahead," growled Hook. "Any man who don't like it can stay here with our friend over there." He waved his hook in the direction of the skeleton. "Anybody choose to stay?"

Not a man moved a muscle.

"Good," smiled Hook. "Then let's go. Them torches won't last forever."

And so they moved deeper into the cave, each man careful to avoid looking at the skeleton nearby.

CHAPTER 17

VOICES

Prentiss led the way, with Tubby Ted stumbling behind. When faced with a decision about which tunnel to take, Prentiss would drop to one knee and feel for their earlier footprints in the muck. He wasn't always sure which footprints he was following—the children's, or the goats'. But one thing was certain: he and Ted were getting farther from the singing voice. After a while, it had faded completely.

Suddenly Prentiss heard something. He stopped. Ted bumped into him.

"Why'd we stop?" said Ted, his voice echoing in the tunnel.

"Shhh!" said Prentiss.

"I think we should keep going," said Ted. "The sooner we're out of here, the better."

"Shut up, Ted!"

"Me?" said Ted. "You're the one making all the noise."

"If you don't shut up," Prentiss hissed, "we're going to stay in here forever and you *won't get any dinner.*"

This was just about the worst thing Ted could imagine. He shut up.

Prentiss stared ahead into the darkness, straining to hear the sound he had heard before.

There it was again.

A man's voice. But it wasn't singing: it was *talking.* And it wasn't behind them, it was *in front of them.*

And it wasn't just one man.

"Prentiss," whispered Tubby Ted.

"It's coming from ahead of us," Prentiss answered, equally quietly. "And it's not the Mollusks because these voices are speaking English."

Both boys listened intently. They couldn't make out exactly what was being discussed—something about "idjits"—but it was clearly English.

"Pirates," Prentiss whispered. "They're coming this way."

Prentiss was going to tell Tubby Ted to turn and run for it. But he didn't have to.

Tubby Ted was already gone.

CHAPTER 18

THE ANGRY MOUTH

SHINING PEARL STOPPED AGAIN. They were deep
in the cave now, having traveled through many
twisting tunnels. The air was colder and wetter.

They now stood in a large, dimly lit chamber
between two narrow tunnels. A reddish glow came
from the tunnel ahead. The path they'd been following clearly led in that direction, towards the
glow.

The light seemed to pull at Thomas and James.

"Why did we stop?" asked Thomas.

"Listen," whispered Shining Pearl.

The boys listened.

"I don't hear anything," said Thomas.

"That's just it! The singing," said James, looking excitedly at Shining Pearl. "It's stopped."

"So, let's go!" said Thomas, looking towards the glow.

"No," said Shining Pearl. "That light looks . . . wrong. It's not sunlight." She sniffed the air. "And the air smells wrong, too."

"It smells fine to me," said Thomas.

"What do you mean, 'wrong?'" said James.

She sniffed again. "It smells stale. It smells like . . ." She stopped.

"Like what?" asked James.

"Like death," said Shining Pearl.

"Death?" said Thomas.

"Yes," she said. "I don't know what it is, exactly. It's just *wrong*."

"But the path goes that way," said Thomas, pointing at the footprints on the cave floor, leading towards the glow ahead.

"It's a trick," said Shining Pearl. "There are lots of footprints on the path we've been following, and they're new. The ones going ahead here are old, and there's just one set. He made those to trick whoever got this far into continuing on down that tunnel. But it's bad. Look here. He doesn't go that way. He steps off the path here. The rest of the prints stop here."

"Wh . . . who's *he?*" said Thomas. "The Goat Taker?"

"I don't know," said Shining Pearl.

"Whoever he is," said James, "if he doesn't go into that tunnel, where *does* he . . ."

Shining Pearl stopped James with an urgent *shhh*.

"Someone's coming," she whispered urgently. "Hide!" She looked frantically around the chamber, then dragged the other two boys into a dark area by the wall, next to the tunnel through which they had entered. Only then did James and Thomas hear it: the sound of feet running towards them. They both held their breath as the footsteps came closer.

Two dark figures, one small and one large, burst out of the tunnel and stepped into the chamber.

"Which way?" said the large one.

"Ted?" said James.

The large figure jumped a foot into the air.

"James!" Tubby Ted said. "Is that you?"

"Yes."

"Thank goodness!" gasped Ted. He and Prentiss bent over, hands on knees, trying to catch their breath.

"Back there," gasped Prentiss, pointing into the tunnel. "Voices."

"The singing?" said James.

Prentiss shook his head violently, drops of sweat spraying from his hair. "Not the singing. *Talking*." He gasped. "English."

"Pirates," gasped Tubby Ted.

"WHAT?" said James and Thomas together.

"They must have seen us go into the cave," said Shining Pearl. She shook her head. "This is bad. This is *very* bad."

"The treasure," said James. "They're after the treasure."

"They're coming," gasped Prentiss, pointing at the tunnel again. "Close."

"Come on," said Ted, starting towards the tunnel at the far end of the chamber.

"Not that way," said James.

"Why not?" said Ted.

"Shining Pearl says that tunnel's stale," said James.

"Stale?" said Ted. "It's *stale*? Who cares? We're

not going to eat it!"

"It's a trap," said Shining Pearl.

"Oh, really?" said Tubby Ted. "And how would you know that?"

"I . . . just . . . know," said Shining Pearl.

"Well," said Prentiss, "if we stay here, the pirates will trap *us*. So what do you suggest we do?"

Shining Pearl looked around the chamber, her eyes straining to see in the gloom.

"Up there," she said, pointing up the steep lava wall to their right. The others looked up and, squinting, saw a small hole shaped like an angry, downturned mouth at the top of the wall.

"You want us to go in *there?*" said Ted. "Are you *crazy?*"

"Do you see any other way out of here?" said Shining Pearl. "That's the way he goes."

"They're coming!" said Thomas.

Sure enough: footfalls, a good many of them, echoed down the tunnel. Coming fast.

"This way," said Shining Pearl, starting to climb the lava wall towards the hole.

"What if you're wrong?" Ted called to Shining Pearl. "What if we get stuck in that hole up there?

What if there are bats or snakes?" He turned to the other boys. "We've followed the path so far. Why change now?"

The footsteps were getting closer. James looked towards the far tunnel, then up at Shining Pearl.

"I trust her," James said. "She got us this far." He began climbing the wall.

One by one, the others followed, with Tubby Ted last in line, muttering.

"She'd better be right," he said.

CHAPTER 19

THE TRAP

Tubby Ted had barely disappeared into the hole when the first pirate, carrying a torch, entered the chamber and stopped. The others were right behind; in a moment the chamber was crowded with sweating men.

"Why did you stop?" barked Hook.

"Ahead there," said the lead man, pointing into the tunnel at the far end. "The light looks a bit odd, Cap'n. The colour, I mean."

Hook stared at the tunnel. He saw what the man meant: the tunnel had a reddish glow.

"That's nothing to worry about," he said. "Nothing at all."

The lead man hesitated.

"MOVE!" bellowed Hook. The torchbearer took a breath and began trotting into the tunnel. The others followed. Some of them noticed that Hook, who had been near the front, now took a spot towards the end of the line. But nobody said anything.

As they moved towards the red glow, the air in the tunnel grew warmer. It also began to have an unpleasant odour.

"Cap'n," Smee called over his shoulder. "The air smells foul."

"KEEP MOVING!" bellowed Hook.

And keep moving they did, though now the air was quite hot, and the stench was almost unbearable. At the front of the line, the lead torchbearer was having trouble breathing. Choking, he stumbled, then fell. His torch clattered ahead of him, rolling on the tunnel floor.

"YOU IDJIT!" shouted Hook from the rear. "GET THAT TORCH BEFORE IT . . ."

He didn't finish his sentence. Instead, he and the

others watched as the torch suddenly dropped and disappeared from sight. A second torch was passed forward. Cautiously, holding their noses against the awful stench, the men crept forward until they saw where the fallen torch had gone—the same place they'd been headed: over the edge of a cliff. It dropped straight down fifty feet to a bubbling, steaming pool of molten lava—the source of the red glow. The tunnel's path, and the footprints, led right to the edge of this cliff.

The air was scalding now; each breath the men took brought hot stinking gas into their lungs. Several of them dropped to their knees, gagging and coughing.

"TURN BACK!" bellowed Hook, realizing they had followed the footsteps into a trap. "TURN BACK, MEN!"

Hook, who was the first to run from the cliff, was the first to make it back to the chamber. One by one, the others stumbled in, coughing.

"They tricked us," fumed Hook.

"Who tricked us, Cap'n?"

"Them boys, you idjit!" said Hook. "They lured us down that tunnel!"

"Ah," said Smee, who had forgotten about the boys. "But where did them boys go, if they didn't go down there?"

Hook wondered that himself.

"Maybe they fell off that cliff," Smee said. "Maybe them boys is dead."

"Don't count on it," muttered Hook. "No . . . they was ahead of us, and now they ain't here. It's like they flew out of here, like bats or something."

"Bats?" said Smee, looking around nervously.

Hook ignored him, his eyes scanning the chamber.

"Aha!" he shouted, pointing at the mouth-shaped hole high up the cavern wall. "Up there!"

Smee squinted in the gloom.

"Begging the cap'n's pardon," he said, "but I don't see nothing up there except that . . . hole."

"That's what I'm talking about, you idjit," said Hook. "They went in that hole!"

"The bats?" said Smee.

"NO, YOU IDJIT!" bellowed Hook. "THE BOYS! COME ON, MEN!"

Urged on by Hook, the men began climbing the lava wall towards the hole. The first to reach it was the man holding the pirates' torch. He stuck the torch inside, then called down to Hook.

"It's another tunnel, Cap'n," he said. "And there's fresh footprints in there."

Hook smiled. "We've got 'em now, men!" he shouted. "And the treasure! After them!"

One by one, the pirates disappeared through the hole and into the upper tunnel. The last to enter was Hook, muttering to himself.

"Thought they fooled me, did they?" he said. "Stupid boys. We'll see who's laughing when I catch up with them."

CHAPTER 20

THE LIFELINE

Shining Pearl stopped short as she emerged from the tunnel. James, Thomas, Tubby Ted, and Prentiss stopped right behind her, seeing, one by one, why she had stopped. For a moment, they simply stared, no one saying a thing.

Then Shining Pearl said, "It's . . . beautiful."

"It doesn't *smell* beautiful," said Tubby Ted, wrinkling his nose.

They were looking down into a vast, gloomy chamber, lit by ghostly sunlight filtering down though two large lava tubes. High above, stalactites hung from the arched ceiling like stone icicles.

Shelves of lava descended, like enormous steps, down to the edge of a cliff that dropped into a gorge of dark water. The water was bubbling and belching some kind of gas—the source of the odour that Ted complained about. Strung across the gorge was a rickety-looking bridge made of rope and boards. It led to the far side, where the lava was pockmarked with large black holes—entrances to a dozen or more tunnels.

"Who do you suppose made that bridge?" asked Prentiss.

"I don't know," said James. "But we're going to have to cross it."

"Not me," said Tubby Ted, eyeing the bridge warily. "I'm not going on that thing."

"Then you'd rather wait here for the pirates?" said Shining Pearl.

As if answering her, a shout echoed from the tunnel behind them.

"They're getting close," said Thomas.

"Hurry!" said Shining Pearl, taking off at a run down the rock shelves and following a worn, twisting path past stalagmites that looked like huge melting candles. She quickly reached the cliff edge, followed by the boys. The five of them studied the bridge. It consisted of four long ropes across the gorge—two below, supporting the boards; and two above, for handholds. The ropes were old and frayed; the boards were cracked and worm-eaten. The bridge hung low in the middle, only a few feet above the stinking liquid bubbling below.

"I don't know about this," said Prentiss.

"We go one at a time," said Shining Pearl. "Who wants to be first?"

None of the boys stepped forward.

"Very well," said Shining Pearl. She grabbed hold of the hand ropes, stretched her right foot forward, then cautiously put her weight onto the first board. The board creaked; the bridge wobbled and swayed. Shining Pearl almost lost her balance but held on. James reached out to pull her back, but she shook her head. "I've got it," she said.

She took another careful step. Then another. Each time the bridge creaked and swayed—but held. As the boys watched anxiously, Shining Pearl made her way slowly across the sagging bridge. Finally she reached the far side, turned, and waved.

As she did, there were more shouts from the

tunnel behind the boys. The pirates were closer now. Much closer.

"We've got to get across quickly," said James. He looked at the other three and decided that since Ted was the heaviest, it would be best to send him over next, before the bridge became any weaker. "Ted," he said.

"But . . . " Ted protested.

"You've *got* to, Ted," said James. "The pirates will be here any moment."

As if to prove the point, a loud shout echoed from the tunnel. Ted didn't need any more persuading. He stepped onto the bridge. He looked down into the water and yelped, yanking on the hand rope so hard that the entire bridge shook and swayed.

"Don't look down!" James said. "Look at Shining Pearl and walk to her!"

Ted did as he was told and started moving. The bridge again creaked and wobbled. But again it held. In a minute, Ted was across the gorge.

The pirates' voices were much closer now, yelling something about a torch.

"Prentiss," said James.

"If it can hold Ted, it can hold two of us," said

Prentiss. "Come on, Thomas!" With Prentiss in the lead, the two boys started across the wobbly bridge.

They'd made it halfway across when Thomas stumbled, yelping as he lost hold of the right-hand rope. He managed to grab the rope again, but yanked it so hard that Prentiss, who had turned to help his friend, lost *his* balance. It happened in an instant: Prentiss slid through the gap between ropes, screaming, and splashed into the gray water below.

James wasn't aware of running out onto the bridge, but in a moment he was next to Thomas. James dropped to his knees and reached down, but Prentiss was just out of reach. He flailed and thrashed, trying desperately to keep his head above the water. His head went under once, then again, and again. Each time he managed to fight back to the surface, but he was tiring.

"Swim to the side!" James called. "To the side!" But Prentiss was unable to do any more than try to stay afloat. James realized that his only hope of saving his friend was to jump in, though he was no great swimmer himself.

He was just about to leap from the bridge when

something slapped the water next to Prentiss. James strained to see what it was. . . .

"A rope!" he called out. "Grab the rope!"

As Prentiss struggled towards the rope, James followed it through the low, gray light with his eyes. It stretched towards the far side of the gorge, well below where Shining Pearl and Tubby Ted were standing.

There, on a ledge near the water, James could

just make out a thin, bent figure with long gray hair and what looked like a beard. He wore only a pair of fraying shorts with holes in them. The man raised his head—it was too dark to see his face—saw James looking at him, and took off. He nimbly bounced up two shelves of rock, climbed straight up like a spider, reached a ledge, and then disappeared into one of the many tunnel entrances.

Directly below, Prentiss reached out and grabbed the rope.

"Pull the rope!" James shouted, as he and Thomas hurried the rest of the way across the bridge.

Shining Pearl, followed by Ted, climbed down to the ledge where James had seen the strange man standing. They found the end of the rope tied to a stalagmite. A moment later, James and Thomas joined them, and together the four of them pulled Prentiss to the edge of the stinking, bubbling water. At last James grabbed Prentiss by the hands and pulled him onto the rock.

"Are you all right?" asked James.

Prentiss coughed up some water, then nodded and said, "I think so."

"You smell awful," said Ted.

Shining Pearl was looking at the rope tied to the stalagmite.

"Who tied this here?" she said. "And who threw the rope?"

"There was a man standing here," said James. "A little man with a long beard. He ran in there." James pointed up to the tunnel he'd seen the man go into.

Suddenly there was a burst of shouts from the far side of the gorge. Torchlight flickered in the mouth of the tunnel.

"We'd better get out of here," said Thomas.

"But which way?" said Ted.

"I say we follow the man," said James. "He helped Prentiss; maybe he'll help us."

He looked at the others; nobody had a better idea, and there was no time left. So, as the pirates entered one side of the cavern, the five children scrambled out the other side, following their mysterious helper.

CHAPTER 21

THE DELAY

ONE BY ONE, THE PIRATES EMERGED from the tunnel. They were down to their last torch now, and there wasn't much light left. But by the dim light of the lava tubes, they saw the last of the boys going into one of the tunnels on the far side of the vast cavern.

"After them!" said Hook.

The men clambered down the rock ledges to the edge of the gorge, where they studied the rickety bridge across the dark, stinking water.

"It don't look safe, Cap'n," said Smee, eyeing the frayed ropes.

"Of *course* it's safe, Smee," said Hook. "I have total confidence in this bridge. Let's go, men! We've nothing to fear!" He pointed at one of the heavier pirates. "You first."

Reluctantly, the man shuffled forward and stepped carefully onto the bridge. He inched forward, pausing every few seconds.

"Move along, there!" said Hook. "Them boys is getting away!"

It took several more minutes for the man to make it across. Hook sent another pirate, then another, each man inching slowly across the gorge. Hook was furious about the delay, but he doubted that the bridge would hold more than one man at a time. And he had no intention of crossing it himself until he was sure it was strong enough.

And so Hook was forced to stand, boiling with impatience, watching his men cross the bridge, while the cursed boys went on ahead, each second getting closer to the treasure.

CHAPTER 22

NO BEARD'S PLAN

SHINING PEARL LED THE BOYS through the pitch black tunnel, feeling her way forward with out-stretched hands. Behind them, they could hear the shouts of the pirates. Ahead was only darkness, though Shining Pearl's nose told her they were moving towards a place where the air was warmer and drier and carried the scent of . . . was that food?

After a few minutes, she saw a dim glow ahead. With each step it grew brighter. Then the tunnel turned sharply right and opened into another large chamber, this one lit by torches along the walls. To the right was a pit of molten lava, glowing fiery red and smoking; the pit was apparently used for cooking, as it was surrounded by bones. To the left was a waterfall, where an underground stream tumbled from the side of the rock into a pool below. But the most striking feature of the chamber stood directly ahead.

"It's a *ship*," said Prentiss.

It was, indeed, a ship. Most of a ship, anyway. It was a ramshackle thing made of weathered boards lashed together with vines. But it was definitely shaped like a ship: there was a bow and a stern, a cabin in the middle, and a mast rising into the gloom of the chamber ceiling.

"What's a ship doing in a cave?" said Thomas.

"Let's ask him," said Shining Pearl.

"Ask who?" said James.

"That man," said Shining Pearl, pointing to the left. There stood the little bearded man. He was holding a rifle. He was pointing it at the children.

"Go back!" he shouted, in a high-pitched, reedy voice. "I helped you back there because you're children and don't know no better. But you don't belong here. Go back!"

Shining Pearl and James exchanged glances. It was James who spoke.

"Sir, we can't go back," he said. "There are pirates that way."

The little man's eyes widened with alarm. "Pirates?" he said. "PIRATES? They've come for the gold!" He looked towards the stern of the makeshift ship, and the children followed his eyes. There, on the deck, sat a moss-covered wooden chest.

"Is that . . . is that the *treasure?*" said James.

"It's gold," said the man. "From the ship *Mariposa*. There was a dozen or more chests like that aboard, all filled with gold, but the rest went to the bottom of the sea. This is the only one that got to this island. I've been guarding it for . . . well, I don't know how long." He lowered the rifle.

"Sir," said Shining Pearl. "Are you . . . the Goat Taker?"

The little man stared at her. "The what?" he said.

"The Goat Taker," she repeated.

"I eat a goat from time to time, to stay alive," said the man. "But that ain't my name. My name is Pesky Lee. Some calls me No Beard."

"But you have a beard," noted Tubby Ted.

The little man looked down at his beard, almost as if he was surprised to see it there. "So I do, so I do," he said. "But No Beard's the name I got as a crewman on this here ship, the *Mariposa*."

"How did the ship get in here?" said James.

"I brung it in, a board at a time," said No Beard. "Took me the longest time, it did. We was wrecked on this island. Storm blew us in, and only a few of us lived. I was the only one who could see. The rest was blind."

"Blind?" said James. "The ship's crew was blind?"

"From the treasure," said No Beard. "It made 'em blind."

"The treasure makes people blind?" Prentiss asked nervously.

"Some people," said No Beard. "Not me, though. I got us to shore and found this cave to hide from the islanders. The other sailors were hurt bad and died soon after. Their bones are guarding the cave now. To keep people away from the gold. I have to guard the gold."

"Why?" said Shining Pearl.

"Why what?" said No Beard.

"Why do you guard the gold?"

No Beard looked surprised. "Why," he said, "because that's my job. I'm a ship's crewman. That there gold is the ship's cargo. I have to protect it, and the ship, until the proper authorities arrive."

"Who would the proper authorities be?" said Shining Pearl.

No Beard frowned. "I honestly don't know," he said. "But I'm waiting for 'em."

"And how would anybody find you in here?" said James.

No Beard frowned again. He turned the rifle around and used the barrel to scratch his beard. "You trying to trick me?" he said.

"And besides," said Shining Pearl, "if the gold makes people go blind, why would anybody want it?"

No Beard frowned yet again. "I never thought of that, neither," he said. "But gold is gold. Though that gold there *has* caused a lot of trouble."

A deep-voiced shout echoed from the tunnel behind them. The five children and No Beard all turned to look.

"Speaking of trouble," said Tubby Ted.

"They'll be here soon," said Thomas.

"Mr. Lee, sir," said Prentiss. "Can you shoot that thing?"

Pesky Lee looked down at the rifle. "'Fraid not," he said. "It don't work at all."

Another shout from the tunnel.

"We have to get out of here," said Shining Pearl. "Right now. Is there another tunnel out?"

"Yes," said Pesky Lee. "It leads back around to the bridge you came over to get here."

"Then let's go," said James. "They'll be here soon."

"James," said Tubby Ted. "I don't think I can run from the pirates much longer."

"Ted, you've *got* to," said James. "Mr. Pesky Lee, sir, which way is the other tunnel?"

"I'll show you," said Lee. "But before we go, maybe you could give me a little help."

"Help with *what?*" said James. "The pirates are almost here!"

A sly smile formed on Lee's face.

"I have an idea," he said, "that might slow the pirates down a bit."

"Well, we'd better do it quickly," said James.

"Follow me," said Pesky Lee.

CHAPTER 23

THE TRAIL OF THE TREASURE

Captain Hook was the last to cross the rickety bridge. When he reached the far side he pointed to the tunnel into which the boys had disappeared.

"Move!" he bellowed.

The first man to enter was the one carrying the torch, which was nearly out. Hook was right behind, followed by Smee and the others. They trotted down a narrow tunnel, which, after fifty feet, took a sudden turn to the right.

The man with the torch stopped so suddenly that Hook ran into his back.

"YOU IDJ—" Hook began, but he stopped in

midbellow when he saw the ramshackle ship looming in the chamber.

Smee saw it next.

"Cap'n," he said, "what's a ship doing in here?"

"I dunno," said Hook, frowning. "But whoever brought it in here must have brought its cargo, too, eh?" Hook's gaze traveled the length of the ship. "Smee," he said, "go read the name."

"What name?" said Smee.

"The *ship's* name, you idjit," said Hook, gesturing impatiently towards the bow.

Smee, watched by the others, trotted towards the ship and peered at the word carved into the wood.

"Cap'n!" he called back. "It says *Mariposa!*"

"I knew it!" said Hook. His glittering dark eyes darted around the chamber. "The treasure must be here somewhere, men. FIND THE TREASURE!"

"Cap'n," said Smee, "if they find the treasure, won't it make 'em blind?"

The men stopped and looked at Hook.

"Don't worry, men!" Hook said. "It'll be in a chest. You're perfectly safe! It's a treasure *chest* you're looking for. Now get to it!"

The men began to search, some poking around

the walls of the massive chamber, and some climbing onto the ship. Hook himself stayed put; he wasn't so sure that what he had told the men about the chest was true.

Five minutes passed, and then ten. Hook tapped his boot impatiently, but his men found no sign of a chest, or gold. Finally Hook had to accept the ugly truth: the gold was not in the chamber.

"It's them boys!" he snarled, spitting onto the chamber floor. "Them boys stole the treasure!"

"But Cap'n," said Smee. "If they took the treasure, how did they get it out of here?"

That stopped Hook short. He'd been so excited about finding the ship that he hadn't thought about where the boys had gone. He frowned, and then it hit him. "There must be another way out!" he said. "Find it, men!"

Again the men searched the huge chamber, but this time they were looking for a second tunnel. It took only a few minutes.

"Cap'n!" shouted a man, waving from behind a massive stalagmite. "It's over here!"

Hook trotted over. The man was standing next to a low opening in the chamber wall.

"Get a torch over here!" shouted Hook. The one they had been carrying had gone out. A crewman grabbed one of the torches from the wall and brought it over. Hook studied the floor in front of the low opening. There was a fresh, smooth trail in the dirt, two feet wide, leading from the ship into the tunnel.

"The chest!" Hook shouted. "They dragged the chest this way. Into the tunnel, men! We've got 'em now!"

With the torchbearer in front, the pirates crawled into the low tunnel. At first it was slow and painful going on hands and knees. But after a few yards the ceiling became higher, until eventually they could stand. They trotted, huffing and puffing through the gloom, following the man with the torch. A half-dozen times he stopped, as the tunnel branched off into two or three paths. Each time the trail of the dragged treasure chest told the pirates which way to go. And each time, they took the left-hand tunnel. To Hook, it felt almost as if they had turned all the way around and were going back in the same direction they'd come from.

His suspicions grew even stronger when his nose

detected an unpleasant but familiar odour. And then, sure enough, they emerged from the tunnel, and found themselves back in the chamber with the rickety bridge across the gorge filled with stinking, bubbling water.

Hook looked down. The trail of the treasure chest led from his feet to the bridge. Hook's gaze followed the trail, then the bridge. He squinted to see in the ghostly light filtering from the lava tubes into the vast chamber. And then his cold heart leaped as he let out a roar of triumph.

For there, in the middle of the gently swaying bridge, stood two children—a boy and a girl.

And next to them, on the rickety boards, sat a chest.

CHAPTER 24

HOOK'S DECISION

Hook's roar filled the chamber. James felt the hair on the back of his neck stand up. From the middle of the creaking bridge, he and Shining Pearl could see the pirates running down to the edge of the gorge.

"Now?" he said.

"Not yet," said Shining Pearl.

James wanted more than anything to start running, to get away from the pirates. Especially the tall one with the hook. He was sure Shining Pearl was scared, too, but if she was, she didn't show it. She stood calmly, watching as Hook, with the rest of the

pirates right behind, reached the end of the bridge—
no more than fifteen yards away. Hook paused, looking at the bridge as if deciding whether it would take
his weight.

"Get ready," said Shining Pearl quietly.

She and James leaned down and grabbed the
handles at either end of the chest.

"Now," said Shining Pearl.

They began to drag the chest away from the
pirates, making a loud THUNK each time it passed
over one of the bridge planks.

James glanced back. Hook was still at the edge of
the bridge. He looked at the chest, then down at the
bridge, then back at the chest moving away. After a

moment of hesitation, Hook made his decision. With another chilling roar, he charged out onto the bridge toward James and Shining Pearl, the other pirates right behind him.

"Now?" James whispered urgently.

"Not quite yet," whispered Shining Pearl, her eyes locked on Hook. "But be ready."

CHAPTER 25

THE GOLDEN WATERFALL

"STOP!" HOOK ROARED. "GIVE ME THAT TREASURE!"

For the first time since they had entered the cave, Hook was leading the way. His greed for the gold had overcome his fear of the rickety bridge, which now was swaying wildly as he lunged forward, struggling to keep his balance.

One by one the other pirates, heartened by their captain's bravery, followed Hook onto the bridge. It groaned and drooped lower towards the water below, but the old ropes were stronger than they looked: the bridge held.

With a snarl of triumph on his face, Hook took another wobbling step forward. He was only five yards from the chest now. The boy and the girl were still trying to drag it away, but it was obviously heavy—all that gold!—and they weren't strong enough to escape with it. Hook saw the fear in the boy's eyes, and it made him happy.

Hook noticed that the girl didn't look frightened; in fact, she almost seemed to be grinning at him.

I'll wipe that smile off your face, thought Hook. He was only a few steps from the chest now. Hook knew there was no chance of the children getting away with it. Apparently they knew it, too; as he took another step towards them, the girl said something to the boy. They both let go of their end of the chest, which dropped onto the bridge with a *clunk*. Then they turned and ran towards the far side of the gorge.

"THAT'S RIGHT, RUN!" Hook shouted. "IT'S OURS, MEN! THE TREASURE'S OURS!" He took another step forward, then another, and he had reached the chest. He examined it: there was no padlock. He reached down and undid the latch. He was about to open the trunk—to gaze upon his gold—when he remembered the Blind Luck curse.

"Smee!" he called. "Open this chest!"

"But Cap'n," said Smee. "Won't it— "

"THAT'S AN ORDER, SMEE!" bellowed Hook.

"Aye," said Smee. Reluctantly, the round little man edged past Hook on the bridge. He put his hand on the chest lid, then paused. "Can I close my eyes, Cap'n?"

"No," said Hook. "Just take a quick look inside and tell me what you see." His voice softened. "A quick look won't do you no harm, Smee."

"Aye, Cap'n," said Smee doubtfully. Slowly, he began to lift the lid. He squinted as it came up.

Hook, on the other hand, was looking away from the chest, not wanting to expose his eyes to the gold. His gaze was aimed past his men, back towards the tunnel they had just come from. As he heard the creak of the chest lid opening, Hook saw something—a movement in the gloom. He squinted, and made out a figure coming down from a rock ledge, heading towards the end of the bridge.

Hook wondered if it was one of the children. Then he saw the figure clearly. It wasn't a child, but a small man, with a long, flowing beard. The man held something in his hand. Hook strained to see what it was. Then he froze.

It was a knife.

"NO!" he shouted, pointing. "STOP HIM!"

The men spun around on the bridge and looked where Hook was pointing. With shouts of fear and rage they started back towards the little man. For a moment he calmly watched them as they stumbled frantically towards him on the swaying bridge. Then, with a smile aimed right at Hook, the man reached the knife down towards one of the bridge hand ropes.

"NOOOO!" screamed Hook.

With an easy swipe, the razor-sharp knife sliced through the rope. Two of the pirates, who'd been holding that particular rope, screamed as they fell into the smelly water.

"I'LL GET YOU!" screamed Hook at the little man. "YOU'LL PAY FOR THIS!"

But the man only smiled as he brought the knife down again. This time he severed the other hand rope. Three more pirates went into the water. The others, Hook included, dropped to their knees or bellies, grabbing at the wooden footboards.

The little man at the end of the bridge bent over

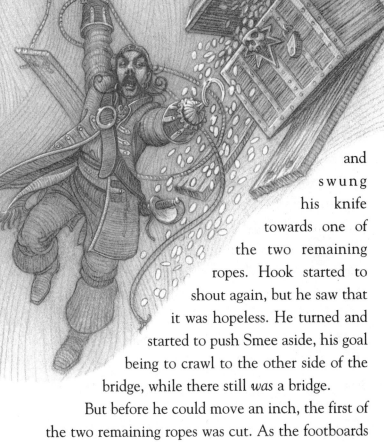

and
swung
his   knife
towards one of
the   two remaining
ropes. Hook started to
shout again, but he saw that
it was hopeless. He turned and
started to push Smee aside, his goal
being to crawl to the other side of the
bridge, while there still *was* a bridge.

But before he could move an inch, the first of
the two remaining ropes was cut. As the footboards
collapsed beneath him, Hook dropped, hanging on
to the lone remaining rope with his good hand.
Directly in front of him he saw the wooden chest fall
sideways, its lid swinging open.

And then, for just an instant, Hook saw it.

Gold. More gold than he'd ever seen in one
place before, and that was a lot of gold. The shiny

coins cascaded from the trunk in a golden waterfall. Hook started to scream with rage, but before a sound could escape his lips, he felt the last rope part, and suddenly he, too, was falling, following his precious treasure down, down into the dark and stinking water.

CHAPTER 26

THE WAY OUT

James and Shining Pearl watched with relief as the pirates plunged into the water. The enormous chamber echoed with the pirates' cries as they splashed about, struggling to reach the sides of the gorge.

"Let's go!" said Shining Pearl.

Up the rock they ran. Shining Pearl hurried past Tubby Ted, Thomas, and Prentiss to take the lead; James took the rear. They fled into one of the tunnel openings.

Thirty yards into the dark tunnel the shouts and cries of the pirates gave way to the shuffle of their own bare feet on the rock of the tunnel floor. They knew the pirates would soon be following them—

and would be very, very angry. But the near-total darkness slowed their pace, with Shining Pearl often forced to feel her way forward with her hands. Each time the tunnel branched, she had to stop and sniff the air, searching for the way out, while behind her the boys waited impatiently.

They passed through a dimly lit chamber where bats—millions of bats, it seemed—hung upside-down from the ceiling. Then they entered another dark tunnel. It branched three times in quick succession; each time Shining Pearl was forced to choose their path in total darkness.

They found themselves in a cramped, smelly tunnel. The ceiling began to lower. James was forced to duck his head, then crouch. Something about this tunnel bothered him. He squeezed past the other boys and caught up to Shining Pearl.

"This isn't right," he whispered. "We didn't come this way."

"Yes, we did," said Shining Pearl, though in fact she was beginning to wonder. "Only it was backwards: we started out bent over, and it got bigger as we went. Everything is reversed, don't forget."

"That was back at Pesky Lee's," said James.

"We didn't have a tunnel like this on the way in."

"I think we did."

"Well, I think you're wrong," he said.

A few yards later the tunnel opened into a small chamber, barely big enough for the five of them to stand in. A small lava tube in the ceiling filled it with a ghostly bluish-gray light. Shining Pearl's eyes scanned the walls.

There was no tunnel opening. They'd reached a dead end.

"Told you," said James.

"Now what?" said Prentiss.

"We turn back," Shining Pearl said grimly. "I'm sorry."

"Don't worry about it," said James, his voice softening. "We'll find the way out."

"But we've lost time," she said. "The pirates . . ."

"We'll be all right," said James. "I'm sure they're still well behind us."

"I hope you're right," said Shining Pearl. She crouched and re-entered the cramped tunnel, followed by Prentiss, Thomas, and Tubby Ted.

James was the last to leave the little chamber.

I hope I'm right, too, he thought.

CHAPTER 27

HOOK'S TRAP

"FASTER!" HOOK BELLOWED. "FASTER!"

With a shove from Hook, the unfortunate crewman selected by him to lead the way stumbled forward in the pitch black tunnel. Several times the man had cried out in pain as he ran into hard rock. Still, Hook prodded him on.

Following Hook, wet and shivering, were Smee and the other men. After the bridge had been cut from under them, they had managed to swim to the edge of the gorge and haul themselves onto the rocks. Now all they wanted was to get out of the cavern.

But Hook wanted more: he wanted the children.

In his mind, he could still see the gold—*his* gold—spilling into the dark water, lost forever. The thought filled him with rage. He was determined to make the children pay for this.

The tunnel had branched several times; each time, Hook knelt and felt the ground, his fingers seeking footprints in the dirt. Each time he had chosen the path that felt as though it had been traveled most recently. From time to time, when a lava tube permitted some light to filter into the cave, Hook noted with satisfaction that he had chosen correctly. He could see many footprints going the opposite way, indicating that this was the path taken by the pirates and the children entering the cave. On top of these, going the same way as Hook and his men were going now, he saw the fresher prints of small, bare feet. These had been left by the children, now heading out. Each time Hook saw these new prints, he allowed himself a small, grim smile. He was still on the trail of the children. He might catch them yet.

"FASTER," he bellowed, giving the man ahead yet another shove.

Onward they went, twisting and turning, until

they came to a huge chamber, dimly lit by lava tubes high overhead. The chamber had a familiar look and smell; the floor was covered with a gooey paste.

Hook's eyes roamed the chamber, taking in the stalagmites rising from the floor, pointing up towards the stalactites hanging high overhead, surrounded by a dark rustling sea of sleeping bats. It looked like there were millions of them.

"I remember this place," Hook said softly.

"Aye, Cap'n," said Smee. "Especially the smell."

"This was the first chamber we came to when we entered," said Hook. "Which means—" He pointed across the vast cavern, at a tall, narrow opening on the other side— "that is the tunnel that leads to the outside."

"So we're almost out, eh, Cap'n?" Smee said happily, starting towards the far side of the chamber.

"Not so fast, Smee," said Hook. He was frowning at the chamber floor.

"What is it, Cap'n?" said Smee.

"The footprints," said Hook. "They ain't here."

Smee looked down at his feet. "Begging the cap'n's pardon," he said, "but there's footprints all around here."

"Yes," said Hook. "But look at the direction of 'em. They're all coming *in*. Do you see any headed *out*? None fresh, you don't. D'you know what that means, Smee?"

"No, Cap'n."

"It means," said Hook, "that they're still in here." He turned and stroked his long moustache. "Somewhere *behind* us."

"Who is?" said Smee.

"The little ones, you idjit," said Hook. "We must have passed 'em somehow. Took a different way. Or maybe it was them that took the wrong turn. Don't matter none: we're ahead of 'em, Smee! We've got 'em!"

"We do?" said Smee, looking around for the children.

"Not yet, you idjit. But sooner or later, they'll head here, to this chamber. And they'll see our footprints leading the way out, to that tunnel over there." He pointed across the chamber at the narrow opening on the far side. "They'll go that way, too, thinking they've made it. But they'll be wrong, Smee. Do you know why?"

"Why, Cap'n?"

"Because we'll be at the end of that tunnel, waiting for them, that's why. Come on, men!"

With the others following—they were only too happy to get out of there—Hook started across the chamber, a smile forming on his face. He may have lost the gold, but he would make the children pay for that. Oh, yes, they would pay.

"Think they outsmarted me, did they?" he muttered as he reached the far tunnel. "We'll see how smart they are when they walk into my trap."

CHAPTER 28

THE BLACK WAVE

SHINING PEARL LED THE FOUR BOYS out of a tunnel into a huge chamber. She glanced around and broke into a smile.

"We're almost out," she said, relief in her voice. "This was the first cave we came to." She pointed towards the high ceiling and the dark, rustling shapes. "Remember the bats?"

"Wish I didn't," said Tubby Ted.

"This is where I first found the skull," said James.

"Wish you hadn't," said Tubby Ted.

"Let's get out of here," said James.

"Wait a moment," said Shining Pearl, looking

down at the confusion of footprints crisscrossing the goo-covered floor.

"What?" said James.

"The men . . . the pirates," she said. "They're *ahead* of us, now. Look, you can see their footprints going that way." She pointed across the chamber to the mouth of another tunnel.

"That's a good thing, right?" said James. "It means they've left the cave."

"I suppose so," said Shining Pearl, frowning.

"So let's go!" said Prentiss.

"Yes!" agreed Thomas. "Let's get out of this stinky cave!"

"I'm hungry," said Tubby Ted.

"All right," said Shining Pearl, still frowning. "But let me go first, all right?"

With the boys following her, she crossed the big chamber. She kept turning her nose this way and that. Halfway across, she held up her hand, stopping the boys. Then she tiptoed over to the entrance of the tall, narrow tunnel that led outside. She sniffed the air again. With a look of deep concern on her face, she returned to the boys.

"We're trapped," she whispered. "There are men in the tunnel waiting for us."

"Are you sure?" said James.

"Yes," she said. "I can smell them."

"You can smell them in this stink?" said Prentiss.

Shining Pearl nodded and said, "I don't think they ever wash."

"But then how do we get out?" asked Thomas.

"I'm hungry," said Tubby Ted.

"Quiet," said James, trying to think. He looked at Shining Pearl. "Do you think there's another way out?" he asked.

She searched the chamber with her eyes, and her nose. "I doubt it," she said. "The only fresh air is coming from that tunnel—and with those men in there, it's not terribly fresh at that."

"Then we *are* trapped," said Prentiss.

"Maybe you are," said a voice from the darkness. "But maybe you're not."

The startled children jerked around to see who had spoken. But there was only darkness and the strange shapes of the stalagmites.

"Who's there?" said James, trying to keep the fear out of his voice.

"Why, it's just me, old Pesky Lee," said the little bearded man, stepping out from behind a stalagmite.

"But . . . but how'd you get here?" said James. "You were on the other side of the water when you cut the bridge down."

"Oh, there's more than one way to get here from there," said Pesky Lee. "Took me longer, is all. I wanted to make sure you children got out all right. I owe you that."

"You owe *us*?" asked James. "Why?"

"You helped me get rid of that gold," said the little man. "All those years, I thought I was keeping the gold; now I see the gold was keeping me. I'm glad to be rid of it. It was evil stuff, that gold. The world is better off without it."

With a pang of guilt, James reached into his pocket. His finger touched the smooth, circular shape of the coin he'd taken from the chest: a souvenir to show Peter. He decided not to mention it to Pesky Lee.

"What do you mean we're not trapped?" said Shining Pearl.

"I mean there might be a way out," said Pesky Lee.

"You mean there's another tunnel?" Prentiss asked hopefully.

"No," said the little man, "just that one." He pointed at the exit tunnel.

"But there's pirates in there!" said Thomas. "Shining Pearl smelled them!"

"So I hear," said Pesky Lee.

"I don't understand," said James. "How're we supposed to get past them, then? They're in there waiting for us!"

Pesky Lee grinned. "Oh," he said, "I think they'll be too busy to worry about you."

"Too busy?" said Shining Pearl. "Too busy with what?"

Instead of answering, Pesky Lee pointed up at the chamber's high ceiling. The children looked up, too. The light coming through the lava tubes was a bit dimmer than it had been a few minutes earlier. The bats seemed more restless. Then, as the children watched, the chamber grew distinctly darker. Some of the bats let go of the ceiling and began flying, their dark shapes flitting back and forth overhead. With each passing second, more bats became airborne. The sound of rustling wings—thousands upon thousands of them—grew louder, then louder still.

"Sunset," said Shining Pearl, suddenly under-standing.

"The Dark Wind," said James.

"Is that what you call it?" said Pesky Lee, raising his voice to be heard over the increasing din. "Me, I calls it the Black Wave. Whatever you call it, it's starting."

"So what do we do?" shouted James, nervously eyeing the bats, now flitting and swooping all around them in a dark, thickening swarm.

Pesky Lee shouted an answer, but the children couldn't hear him. His voice was drowned out by the beating of a million wings.

CHAPTER 29

SCREAMS OF RAGE

"CAP'N," SAID SMEE, looking nervously back into the tunnel, "what's that sound?" He ducked as the dark shape of a bat shot past his head.

"Quiet, Smee!" hissed Hook. "That must be the children. They'll be coming out any minute now. You men be ready!"

Hook had posted his men just inside the vines that covered the entrance to the cave. Hidden in the shadows, they were supposed to be ready to pounce on the escaping children. But at the moment all the men were, like Smee, looking with alarm into the tunnel as the sound grew louder and more bats flew out.

"Beggin' the cap'n's pardon," said Smee, "but that don't sound like children."

Hook was reluctant to admit it, but Smee was right: it didn't sound like children at all. It sounded more like a typhoon. More bats were coming out now, and more and more, and still more, filling the entire tunnel, swarming around the pirates. Hook waved his hook at them, trying to fend them off, but they kept coming, more and more. Turning away from the river of bats, he saw his men panicking—some stumbling out of the cave, some crawling, some simply curled up on the tunnel floor covering their faces with their arms.

"GET UP, YOU COWARDS!" Hook screamed. "GET UP!" But by then the men could not hear him over the roar of the wings.

Hook was the only one to remain standing at the cave entrance. But he could no longer see anything. Bats—thousands and thousands—swirled past him, unaffected by his screams of rage.

CHAPTER 30

CAUGHT

Pesky Lee was shouting at Shining Pearl. His mouth was only an inch from her ear, but she could barely hear him. The sound of the bats was terrifyingly loud, made still louder by the echo in the vast chamber.

". . . HAND!" he was yelling. "MY HAND!"

Finally understanding, Shining Pearl took his outstretched hand. Pesky Lee then grabbed her free hand and put it in Thomas's hand. With effort, the little bearded man got the children to form a chain—Prentiss holding onto Thomas, Ted holding onto Prentiss, and James last in line. Once they were all connected, Pesky Lee began tugging them towards the exit tunnel, the children ducking their heads and moving with difficulty as they tried to avoid the swift dark shapes swarming past them.

Swept along by the river of bats, they reached the exit tunnel, where, impossible as it seemed, the noise became even louder. Darkness was total now; the children were too terrified to scream as they entered the tunnel. Every inch was filled with bats, their leathery wings thrashing against the children's faces, their furry bodies brushing against the children's bare arms and legs. Engulfed by the swirling tide of flying creatures, Pesky Lee and the children stumbled forward. Shining Pearl tried to drop to her knees to escape the bats, but Pesky Lee yanked her forward, keeping her on her feet, trying to keep the children moving inside the terrible, dark wave.

Then, gently, the tunnel bent left, and suddenly it was no longer pitch black. Ahead of them, through the flurry of bats, Pesky Lee and the children saw the deep gray curtain of twilight. . . . The sky! They were almost out!

Together, with the bats still swirling all around them, but with hope in their hearts, they staggered forward, still holding hands. Pesky Lee, looking ahead, stumbled over something. Shining Pearl, right behind, looked down at it and screamed.

It was a pirate. He was lying on the ground, curled into a ball, sobbing in terror; he didn't seem to notice Pesky Lee and the children. They stepped over him, and, looking around, saw several more pirates, also lying on the ground, covering themselves up against the bats.

"HURRY!" shouted Pesky Lee, yanking the children forward, wanting to get them out of the cavern while the bats still provided cover. And hurry they did, lunging forward, until Pesky Lee felt fresh air on his face and knew he was outside of the cave. Behind him, one by one, came the others, with James the last to reach the cave mouth, where he raised his head to look at the night sky . . .

. . . and felt a hand grab his ankle.

The grip was so tight he screamed in pain. Down he went, letting go of Ted's hand. He tried to kick his leg free, but the grip only tightened. He looked forward; Pesky Lee and the others had disappeared into the cloud of bats swirling from the cave. He kicked again and heard a roar of pain and

anger from behind him, but still the grip held. He was caught.

James turned towards his captor and saw the face he least wanted to see in all the world: Hook.

The pirate was on his knees, his hand gripping James's ankle, his hook slicing the air, fending off the bats. With another roar he yanked James's leg, sliding the boy towards him. James was now on his back, looking straight up at the pirate captain, who stared back down with a look of pure hatred in his blazing black eyes. Ignoring the bats now, the pirate pinned James to the ground with one hand and held his hook in front of the boy's face, so James could see its gleaming, razor-sharp edge, its needle-sharp point.

The look of terror in James's eyes pleased Hook. He smiled, revealing a crooked row of jagged brown teeth beneath his thick, black moustache.

"Thought you'd got away, did you, *boy?*" Hook said, raising his voice to be heard over the still-steady roar of the bats. "You lost my gold, boy. MY GOLD!" He raised the hook over his head, preparing to bring it down.

"Not all of it!" shouted James. "It's not all lost!"

Hook paused, his hook suspended in the air. "What do you mean, boy?"

"There's still some gold left!" said James, desperation in his voice.

"YOU'RE LYING, BOY!" said the pirate, raising his hook again.

"No!" cried James. "There's some gold left, I swear it!"

"Where is it, then?" said Hook, greed overcoming his desire for revenge. "TELL ME WHERE IT IS, BOY! IF YOU'RE LYING, I'LL . . ."

"Here!" said James, reaching into his pocket and pulling out the gold coin. He held it up to Hook. "Take it! It's yours!"

Hook took his hand from James and grabbed the coin. He held it up to his face and smiled.

And then he screamed.

"My eyes!" he shouted, hurling the coin away. "MY EYES! I CAN'T SEE!"

With a furious thrust, he brought the hook down. But instead of hitting flesh, the hook plunged deep into dirt, barely missing James, who had rolled sideways just in time. As the pirate strained to yank his hook out of the ground, James scrambled to his feet.

"I'LL GET YOU, BOY!" Hook screamed, yanking the blade from the ground and swinging it around wildly. "I'LL GET YOU!"

But James was out of reach, running through the swirling cloud of bats towards his friends, leaving the pirate captain screaming and slashing blindly at the air.

CHAPTER 31

WARM AND SAFE

SHINING PEARL LED THE WAY down to the Goat
Meadow, followed by Prentiss, Thomas, Tubby Ted,
James, and—bringing up the rear—Pesky Lee. The
little bearded man had insisted on following the
children, in case the pirates came back.

There was little danger of that. The pirates had
stumbled frantically away from the cave, swiping the
air to be rid of the bats. They were now on the way
back to their side of the island, Smee leading
Captain Hook, whose sight was slowly returning. He
could be heard for a half mile bellowing in rage over
his lost treasure.

That had been half an hour ago. Now the pirates were long gone, and the bats scattered into the quiet night air. The children made their way down to the meadow by the light of the rising moon. As Shining Pearl reached the meadow's edge, she saw the dark shapes of sleeping goats. Then she saw another, larger shape coming towards her. She tensed, knowing who it was, even if she hadn't recognized the large shape. She let out a cry of relief.

"Father!" she said, running forward and jumping into the strong arms of Fighting Prawn, chief of the Mollusk tribe. Little Scallop followed behind him, along with four Mollusk braves, all holding spears.

Fighting Prawn picked Shining Pearl up and hugged her tight for what seemed like a very long time. Then he set her down and gave her a disapproving look that, even seen in the twilight, meant a lecture was coming. Out of his mouth flowed a rapid series of sharp grunts and clicks. Shining Pearl bowed her head.

"What's he saying?" James asked Little Scallop.

"He's mad at her for going into the Cave of the Dark Wind," answered Little Scallop.

"That's right," said Fighting Prawn, switching to

English, and giving James an equally unhappy look. "I'm very disappointed in you, too, James."

"I'm sorry, sir," said James. "But there was a treasure in there, and—"

"Treasure?" interrupted Fighting Prawn. "What good would treasure do you if the Goat Taker had gotten you?"

"But there is no Goat Taker!" said Shining Pearl.

"What do you mean?" said Fighting Prawn. "Something has been taking the goats."

"Yes," said Shining Pearl, "but it's not . . . I mean, he's not . . . I mean—" She looked around. "Where'd he go? Where's Pesky Lee?"

The children looked around; the little man wasn't there.

"Pesky Lee!" shouted Shining Pearl. "Please come out! Nobody will hurt you!"

There was a rustle in the tall grass, and then Pesky Lee, who'd been hiding from the Mollusk warriors, stood up.

"Here's Pesky Lee," he said, nervously.

The Mollusks, spears ready, took a few threatening steps towards the little man.

"No!" said Shining Pearl, jumping between the

spears and Pesky Lee. "He helped us! He saved us from the pirates!"

Fighting Prawn held up a hand, stopping the warriors. He turned to Shining Pearl.

"The pirates were in the cave?" he said.

"Yes," said Shining Pearl.

"Tell me exactly what happened," he said.

So Shining Pearl told him the whole story—about the skull, the ship, the gold, the pirates, Pesky Lee, and the bats. When she was done, Fighting Prawn nodded once, then spoke.

"I'm still disappointed with you children for going into the cave," he said. "Especially you, James—you put your friends in terrible danger."

James bowed his head.

"But you also showed great bravery," he said, getting small smiles from both James and Shining Pearl. "And," he continued, "thanks to you, the mystery of the Goat Taker has been solved." He turned to Pesky Lee.

"Mr. Lee," he said, "you saved my daughter's life. You don't need to be afraid of me or anyone else on this island. And you are welcome to take a goat whenever you need one."

Pesky Lee tugged at his beard. "If it's all the same to you," he said, "I'd rather not. Truth is, I'm sick of goat."

"Well then," said Fighting Prawn, "come to our village. We have fish and coconuts and many other good things to eat. You're welcome to as much as you want, whenever you want."

"I'm hungry," said Tubby Ted.

Fighting Prawn laughed. "I imagine you're all hungry, after the day you've had. Mr. Lee, would you care to join us, and the children, for a meal?"

"That'd be lovely," said Pesky Lee.

So they walked down through the moonlight to the village, where they had a fine feast. The children told and retold the story of the day's adventure, except for Ted, who mostly chewed and swallowed. Later, feeling warm and safe, they fell asleep by the fire.

The last thought James had, as his eyes closed, was how jealous Peter would be when he found out what he'd missed.